She bra... questio... another word of what had happened. But instead, he simply...pulled her into his arms silently.

The gesture startled her as much as the brief brush of his lips had back in their prison cabin before they'd broken free. She was convinced that he couldn't stand her, yet this was the second time he wanted to comfort her and did so with an intimate gesture.

She pulled back and looked up into his face. "Why are you doing this?"

"Damned if I know. I didn't exactly plan it."

"So what, you took me into your arms against your will?"

He grinned at her. "I'm a handsome prince, aren't I? I'm used to beautiful women throwing themselves at me."

He was impossible. Impossible to argue with, impossible to ignore, impossibly handsome. Beautiful, cultured, high-born women probably did throw themselves at him on a daily basis.

She braced herself for more questions, determined not to speak another word of what had happened. But instead, he simply... pulled her into his arms silently.

[illegible]

DANA
MARTON

ROYAL CAPTIVE

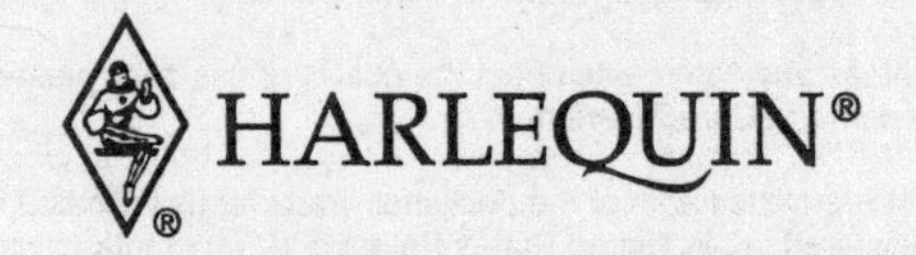

TORONTO • NEW YORK • LONDON
AMSTERDAM • PARIS • SYDNEY • HAMBURG
STOCKHOLM • ATHENS • TOKYO • MILAN • MADRID
PRAGUE • WARSAW • BUDAPEST • AUCKLAND

With many thanks to Allison Lyons

Recycling programs
for this product may
not exist in your area.

ISBN-13: 978-0-373-69479-2

ROYAL CAPTIVE

This edition published by arrangement with Harlequin Books S.A.

For questions and comments about the quality of this book please contact us at Customer_eCare@Harlequin.ca.

www.eHarlequin.com

Printed in U.S.A.

ABOUT THE AUTHOR

Dana Marton is the author of more than a dozen fast-paced, action-adventure romantic suspense novels and a winner of the Daphne du Maurier Award of Excellence. She loves writing books of international intrigue, filled with dangerous plots that try her tough-as-nails heroes and the special women they fall in love with. Her books have been published in seven languages in eleven countries around the world. When not writing or reading, she loves to browse antiques shops and enjoys working in her sizable flower garden where she searches for "bad" bugs with the skills of a superspy and vanquishes them with the agility of a commando soldier. Every day in her garden is a thriller. To find more information on her books, please visit www.danamarton.com. She loves to hear from her readers and can be reached via e-mail at DanaMarton@DanaMarton.com.

Books by Dana Marton

HARLEQUIN INTRIGUE

806—SHADOW SOLDIER
821—SECRET SOLDIER
859—THE SHEIK'S SAFETY
875—CAMOUFLAGE HEART
902—ROGUE SOLDIER
917—PROTECTIVE MEASURES
933—BRIDAL OP
962—UNDERCOVER SHEIK
985—SECRET CONTRACT*
991—IRONCLAD COVER*
1007—MY BODYGUARD*
1013—INTIMATE DETAILS*
1039—SHEIK SEDUCTION
1055—72 HOURS
1085—SHEIK PROTECTOR
1105—TALL, DARK AND LETHAL
1121—DESERT ICE DADDY
1136—SAVED BY THE MONARCH†
1142—ROYAL PROTOCOL†
1179—THE SOCIALITE AND THE BODYGUARD
1206—STRANDED WITH THE PRINCE†
1212—ROYAL CAPTIVE†

*Mission: Redemption
†Defending the Crown

CAST OF CHARACTERS

Istvan Kerkay—Fourth in line to the throne. A cultural anthropologist/archaeologist who feels more comfortable digging in the ground than talking to people. When he suspects that a onetime thief has taken off with the Valtrian crown jewels, he goes after her with a vengeance.

Lauryn Steler—Born into the illegal art-trafficking business, Lauryn has worked hard to establish an honest life since her father's death. But few people are willing to give her a chance, including the stubborn—and gorgeous—prince.

George Bellingham—An agent who deals in stolen artifacts, working out of his base on Cyprus. When he smells a good deal, nothing stands in his way.

Berk and Canda—Two rival crew bosses with reputations for pulling off the most difficult heists.

The Freedom Council—A secret group of prominent businessmen whose sole purpose is to destroy the royal family and break the country into small republics that they could rule individually.

Arpad Kerkay—The Crown Prince is a colonel in the air force. Since the queen is ill, he will soon inherit the crown.

Miklos Kerkay—Second to the throne. He is an army major and a happily married man.

Janos Kerkay—Third in line to the throne. He is an economist and a superb yachtsman who regularly wins golf championships.

Lazlo Kerkay—The "Rebel Prince" is a successful entrepreneur whose company builds race cars. He is happily married to Mildas, formerly a New York matchmaker, and the only woman who could ever tame him.

Benedek Kerkay—Lazlo's twin and the youngest prince, he has two passions: architecture and his wife, Rayne Williams, the opera-singing sensation.

Chapter One

The five men in the back of an unmarked van across the park from the Valtrian Royal Palace maintained radio silence. They were crowded by a wall of instruments, ignoring the dead body at their feet, watching the feed from a button camera that panned one checkpoint after another as its wearer passed through them.

Then the gilded, magnificent reception room of the palace came on the screen at last, looking exactly like the postcards vendors sold all over the city.

"Boss's in. We're good to go," the oldest of the men said, then clapped the rookie on the shoulder. "We'll be in an' out before they know what hit 'em."

The mood in the air was tense but optimistic as they checked their weapons.

"ANYONE BUT HER." Prince Istvan nestled the stash of two-hundred-year-old documents back into their leather pouch, then a ziplock bag and a protective box, careful not to damage the brittle paper. He shoved the copy he was making by hand into the inside pocket of his jacket. Every time he began work on the Maltmore diary, someone or something interrupted him. His office, located deep inside the palace, was supposed to be his sanctuary. He resented this latest intrusion, even if by his own brother.

Janos lifted a one-of-a-kind, eleventh-century medicine vial and turned it over, tapping the bottom with his fingernail while eyeing the rest of the curiosities on the desk. "She's already here. How was Brazil?"

"Loud." Istvan grabbed the artifact with his white-gloved hands and set it back on its special stand. He'd trained the staff to respect his wishes and keep their hands to themselves. But nothing was sacred to his brothers, who felt free to waltz in and rifle through centuries-old treasures as they used to ransack through each other's toy chests three decades back.

Janos—economist, two-time golf champion and superb yachtsman—was moving toward a side table and eyeing a medieval broadsword that had been brought in only that morning by a farmer who was digging a new well. A lot of discoveries were made like that. Istvan was itching to stop by for a look of his own. He had the farmer's invitation and full permission. All he had to do was find some time later in the week.

He could probably clear Friday morning, he decided as he came around his desk and deftly stepped between his brother and the sword.

Janos, older by a year, adjusted his impeccable tuxedo and fixed him with a look as he opened his mouth to speak.

Here it comes. The speech on how Istvan should pay as much attention to living things as inanimate objects. He heard that enough from his family to be able to recite it by heart. He shoved his hands into his jeans pockets, the only one of the royal brothers who would ever dress so low. He caught plenty of hell for it, too, the tabloids regularly mocking him as the worst-dressed of the princes. As if he didn't have bigger things to worry about.

"What are you going to do about her?" Janos asked, skipping the lecture, which was unlike him. He probably had the latest trouble in the financial markets on his mind.

"I'm not sending for her today." He'd decided that as soon as he had arrived that morning and was alerted to her presence at the palace. He was hoping to get out to the old palace wall before lunch to check on a small excavation there, one among two dozen projects he had going on simultaneously. "Maybe tomorrow. Or the day after."

His time was in even shorter supply than usual. The last of the summer sunshine poured in the oversize windows, reminding him that whatever excavations he wanted to finish this year, he better get on it. Soon the fall rains would slow all open-air digs to a crawl, then the winter freeze would stop surface work altogether until spring.

An amused look flashed across his brother's face. "I don't think she's the type to wait to be sent for."

"I know exactly what type she is," he muttered under

his breath then, watching Janos closely for any clues, asked, "Have you met her?" Janos was a fairly good judge of women, with experience that outpaced Istvan's by at least five to one.

"Have not had the pleasure. But I've been told she's already at work in the treasury. Seems very diligent. Certainly an interesting woman from what I hear." His brother moved on to the glass-front display cabinets. "Your office is starting to look like a warehouse again. Time to send a few boxes over to the museum. Learn to let go. Anyone ever told you that?"

Istvan was thinking about how long he could put off the meeting without appearing inexcusably rude, so his brain caught up with his brother's words a few seconds late. "What treasury?" His muscles jerked, and he nearly knocked over a vase by his elbow, a unique piece that had taken the better part of a month to piece together.

He steadied the copper coil stand, his jaw muscles tightening. "Who authorized it?"

"There's only one treasury at the royal palace. And I believe Chancellor Egon gave her the go-ahead. Did I tell you I finally got a golf GPS? Gives accurate distance to any key point on any golf course." He was grinning like a kid at Christmas. "You should get one."

Istvan strode for the door, his mind as far from golf as possible. "Come." He gestured with impatience when he was forced to wait for Janos to follow. Once they were both out, he turned the key in the door, then pocketed it—he didn't like the way Janos had been looking at that sword—then he took off down the hallway as if the devil was after him.

But the devil was ahead of him, in fact.

"It could be worse," Janos called out with undisguised glee. "The Chancellor could have brought her here to make you marry her."

He barely paid attention to his brother's words. The Chancellor had given up his mad quest to see all the princes married just to gain good publicity for the royal family. The unfortunate marital consultant who'd come all the way from New York City to see Lazlo settled had eaten poison meant for the prince and nearly died of it. All worked out well at the end; Lazlo married her in a stunning turn of events. But the Chancellor lost his taste for matchmaking after that.

Which meant the remaining three Kerkay brothers who were still single could breathe easy for now. Although, to be fair, Istvan almost rather would have been forced to marry than be forced to share his treasures with *that* woman. Because he didn't plan on falling in love again, an arranged marriage would have suited him fine. For certain, he wouldn't put up such a fuss as Lazlo had when his matchmaker arrived. When the time came for Istvan to take that blow, he'd take it on the chin and be done with it.

He strode across the reception room without looking in the floor-to-ceiling Venetian mirror, a gift to one of his ancestors from a sixteenth-century doge, but made a mental note that a minor repair job of the silver backing still had to be scheduled. He pulled off his white cotton gloves and shoved them into his pocket, exited the room and ran down the long hallway that led to the treasury—to hell with decorum.

The guards at the door snapped their heels together in greeting. He went through, nodding to the next set of guards in the antechamber. Then he burst through the door to the treasury proper, a large hall with tables covered in velvet, giant bank safes lining one wall, another hosting hundreds of secured deposit boxes.

Priceless rugs, left behind by the Turkish invasion four hundred years ago, were kept in a climate-controlled chamber, along with some elaborately studded and painted war chests. Artwork that wasn't on display at the moment in the palace was kept in a side room, exhibited there in all its splendid glory.

"Your Highness." Chancellor Egon came forward and made the introductions.

"Your Highness." The woman measured up Istvan as she did a rather understated curtsy. She wore white gloves meant to protect museum artifacts, identical to the ones he'd just taken off.

Probably so she wouldn't leave fingerprints. She wasn't fooling him. Once an art thief, always an art thief—he believed that with his whole heart. As far as he was concerned, Lauryn Steler was only one small step above a tomb raider, which had been her father's sordid occupation, in fact.

She and her kind stood for everything he spent his life fighting against.

"Miss Steler." Greeting her politely took effort, but

good manners had been hammered into all six princes at an early age. He did stop short, however, of telling her that she was welcome at the palace.

"Chancellor Egon was about to show me the coronation vault." She beamed, either not noticing the slight or choosing to ignore it.

Fury that had been rising inside him now bubbled dangerously close to the surface. "How kind of him." His voice had enough edge to cut through the seven-layer titanium alloy that still stood between her and his heritage, the sacred symbols of his country and his family.

The Chancellor stiffened and took a step back, giving him a worried look. "Your Highness, I was merely—"

"I'll take over here. You may leave."

"Certainly, Your Highness." The Chancellor backed out without argument. He'd lost a lot of his bluster and bossiness after the mishap with Lazlo. He wasn't exactly malleable, but he no longer butted heads with the princes over every little thing either.

The woman was still politely smiling. Her mouth was a tad too wide to be called aristocratic, but nevertheless, some people would have found her face pleasant. She didn't seem to have caught a single whiff of doom in the air.

"This is exciting," she said.

Either she was beyond belief impertinent or incredibly dense. Given her reputation, Istvan didn't think it was the latter.

"Isn't it?" He didn't bother forcing a smile, welcoming

or otherwise. "I imagine it's the first time you've seen something like this."

"Yes, yes, it is." Her green-gold eyes looked a little too wide with innocence.

Of course, she'd been in a treasury before. In Portugal, he seemed to remember now something he'd heard about her a while back. If half the rumors about her were true, she'd been the best art thief who had ever lived.

She certainly dressed like a cat burglar. A pair of tight-fitting black slacks covered her long legs, her black short-sleeved shirt leaving her toned arms bare. She was as perfectly proportioned as a painting by the grand masters, her eyes mesmerizing, her skin translucent, her lines magnificent. Her copper hair was pulled into a sleek ponytail to make sure it didn't get in her way.

The closer he looked, the easier he could see how she'd bewitched many of her victims in the past, even poor Chancellor Egon who'd been taken by her enough to open the treasury doors, of all things. *No fool like an old fool,* his father had been fond of saying.

Good thing Istvan was always a lot more interested in what lay below the surface of things. And in her heart of hearts, Lauryn Steler was a thief, the worst kind of villain. He didn't care if the whole world had forgotten that. *He* wouldn't.

"I've already seen a few pieces I would like to take," she told him as if she were at one of those abominable wholesale outlets of her country that sold mass-produced goods in batches.

"I'm sure you have."

If she weren't a consultant for the Getty Center in Los Angeles, one of the most respected museums in the world, his answer would have been, *Over my dead body.* But the board at the Getty had asked for a loan of Valtrian artifacts for a special exhibit. Then the treasure would embark on a trip, residing for three months each in the top-twenty most-prominent museums of the world.

Chancellor Egon had made cultural exchange his new quest. If he couldn't use another row of royal weddings to cheer up the people and raise the country's visibility abroad, then he would do it by parading Valtria's past all over creation. A very bad idea, Istvan had been saying from the beginning, but somehow the Chancellor gained the Queen's approval anyway.

Of course, as ill as the Queen was some days, the Chancellor could probably manipulate her into any agreement. Istvan had said as much to Arpad, but his eldest brother brushed off his concerns. The Crown Prince fully trusted the Chancellor.

Maybe he should have left the conference in Brazil and come back to the palace sooner, Istvan thought now, looking at the woman, still unsure what to do with her. She moved with sinuous grace as she considered the display cases, wandering away from him as if pulled by a magnet toward his country's treasures.

"Magnificent," she said with awe that didn't seem phony.

"And protected by state-of-the-art security," he mentioned in a note of forced nonchalance, not at all approving of that throaty, sexy voice of hers that didn't go with her sleek, crisp appearance.

Her voice belonged to a seductress swathed in silk in a candle-lit boudoir. He blinked that ridiculous image away. He didn't think Miss Steler spent much time reclining on satin pillows. He could, however, see her rappelling from high ceilings, or jumping roofs and disappearing with her latest loot strapped to her back, nearly invisible in the night.

He had a feeling that if quizzed, she could tell him the exact number and location of every security camera in the room, in addition to the content and worth of each display. The Getty sending her was a stunning oversight.

Their excuse was that none of her past transgressions could be proven. That they couldn't punish her for her father's sins. That even if she had a shady past once, she was reformed now, one-hundred-percent trustworthy and the best in the business.

"Shall we?" she was asking with unbridled optimism, nodding toward the safe door that protected the crown jewels.

He wished he could say, *When hell freezes over.* Instead, he stepped up to the iris scanner. "Istvan Kerkay," he said for the voice recognition software. And with a soft hiss, the hydraulic lock opened.

The lights inside came on automatically. He motioned for her to proceed first. As outraged as he was, he was still a gentleman.

She gave a soft gasp.

He didn't blame her. The sight had the same effect on him, and he'd been in here hundreds of times. In glass cases that lined the small chamber were the most important treasures of the kingdom. The crown without which there could be no coronation and no new king. The specter. The Queen's tiaras. A ceremonial sword with a gold-and-diamond handle that he remembered his father wearing when he'd been a kid. A robe woven from threads of gold, once worn at coronations but now put away for all prosperity as it had become too fragile to even touch.

There were other treasures. The most important of the Queen's jewels took up one long case. Another held the signet rings of all the old kings.

She moved to stand in front of the main case.

"None of those will be going anywhere, you understand," he told her. "There's a law forbidding any of the coronation jewels to leave the country." If the Queen traveled to visit other heads of state, she usually took one of the lesser crowns or a simple tiara.

She nodded, but seemed distracted, as if she'd barely heard him. From the corner of his eye, he caught her fingers twitching. She was flexing her hands inside her gloves.

Probably thinking that he'd open one of the cases and let her take something out for closer examination. *The temerity of her—* He stepped back, ready to get her out of the vault. Everything about her being in there shouted *wrong* and went against his most basic instincts. "So now that we're done here..."

That green-gold gaze flew to him, still filled with awe. Her delicate nostrils were trembling. "One more minute, please." She wasn't exactly begging, but she was close to it. There was a luminous quality to her all of a sudden, as if what she was seeing was lighting her up from the inside.

He understood exactly how she felt and resented having even this small thing in common with her. But he couldn't deny that he had felt like this dozens of times in the past when he stood over a new discovery. No amount of time would have been enough. And he wasn't about to indulge her, in any case.

"Maybe another time," he said, but thought, *Not as long as I live and breathe.*

She walked out as if leaving physically hurt her, moving as slowly as possible, glancing back frequently.

He sealed the door behind them and made a show of setting the locks, then pointed toward the back of the treasury. "I was thinking a few paintings and dresses." A number of those had been severely damaged over the centuries and had to be extensively restored. Save a few square centimeters here and there, little of them was original.

She looked back toward the vault and drew a deep breath before turning her attention to him. "I understand that you're reluctant to let anything go. But we have to keep in mind that whatever I take to the Getty will also be going around the world to represent your country."

She was making a play on his pride. Smart, but she

wasn't going to trap him as easily as that. "Be that as it may, the safety of the artifacts is my first concern."

"And mine, as well." Her chin came up, her eyes challenging him to bring up her past.

Of course, she could easily dismiss anything he said as malicious rumor. A prince did not stoop to repeating rumors in any case. He said nothing.

"I was thinking some of the artifacts left behind by the Brotherhood of the Crown," she told him after a moment, wiping the small, triumphant smile off her face so fast he might have imagined it. "They make a compelling story. Eight brothers, princes, coming together to save their country. They were brave and dashing. It's very romantic. I think their story is perfect to introduce Valtria to an American audience."

Definitely not artifacts of the Brotherhood. She was beginning to give him a headache. He'd returned from an overseas trip only that morning. He was tired and irritable, a dozen things clamoring for his immediate attention. He didn't have time for this.

"We have plenty of chances to discuss all that later. Now that you've seen the treasury, you should probably go and see the Royal Museum." Let her be somebody else's problem for a while. Her charm couldn't do much harm over there. She could ask for all she wanted, and the museum director could promise anything she could hoodwink out of him. All final decisions on the items that would go on tour were Istvan's. He could and would overrule any promise that felt injudicious to him.

She threw a disappointed, longing glance toward the

wall of safety boxes and the other vaults, then gathered herself. "Of course. The museum is on my itinerary." She looked around one more time. "Do you have some sort of an inventory of everything that's in here?"

"Color catalogs." A fine set. He'd put them together.

"I would love to take a look."

"I'll have them sent over to your hotel." After he decided which catalogs she could see.

He called a guard to escort her to the museum and stay with her. Then he took one last glance at the room, to make sure nothing was missing, before he headed back to his office.

But when he was sitting at his desk at last, ready to tackle his correspondence, he realized he was completely exhausted. He'd flown home on the red-eye from Brazil where he'd given an address at a conference as the head of the European Society of Social Anthropology. He could never sleep on anything that moved, forget the first-class fully reclining seats of the plane. He had motion sickness, worse than the plague for someone who traveled as much as he did.

He glanced at his watch. Maybe he could squeeze in thirty minutes of rest. He was used to taking short breaks like this when out in the field on a dig. They often had to work around the clock to beat collapsing tunnels or bad weather.

Going up to his suite would have taken too much time, so he simply let his head rest against the back of the chair, stretched his legs in front of him and folded his hands over his abdomen. But far from refreshing, his sleep was restless, his dreams disturbing.

He woke to desperate knocking on his door some time later, blinked hard while he ran his fingers through his hair, then adjusted the collar of his shirt as he sat up straight. Cleared his throat. "Come in."

Chancellor Egon burst through the door, breathing as hard as if he'd been doing laps around the grand ballroom. His eyes were wide with panic. "Miss Steler is missing."

"Is she now?" And good riddance. Things were looking up. She had probably assessed their security system, realized it was beyond her and given up whatever thieving plans she'd been nursing. Istvan's heart was suddenly lighter as he looked toward the upcoming week.

"We—" The Chancellor wrung his hands, apparently thinking this was some great tragedy. He was rather attached to the idea of the artifacts touring, his flying in for each opening and giving one of his interminable speeches on Valtrian glory. "We—"

"What is it?" Istvan glanced at the antique clock on the wall and realized he'd slept a lot longer than he'd meant to. His gaze slid to Amalia's photo in its silver frame under the clock, and his heart gave a painful thud as always. God, how he missed her.

He focused back on the Chancellor, who was still hemming and hawing. "Anything else?" He didn't have all day to waste on Miss Steler.

The Chancellor went pale as he said, "Your Highness, I'm afraid— I have to inform you—" He took a deep breath and spit it out at last. "I've come from the treasury. We can't find the crown jewels either."

Chapter Two

"I want the security tapes." Istvan paced the room. He wanted progress, and was getting anything but. No more than half an hour could have passed since he'd first received the news from the Chancellor, but, without answers, every minute of that time seemed unbearably long.

He was at the security offices on the basement level of the palace with Miklos, Janos and Arpad. Benedek was on a world tour with Rayne, his opera-diva wife, in South Africa at the moment. Lazlo was still on his honeymoon on some undisclosed Mediterranean island.

"There's no security footage." Miklos was seething, as well, ignoring the worried looks of some of the security personnel in the next room. He could be intimidating when angered, something that came from decades of army life. He could stare down a full platoon if needed. No doubt, he'd had already taken the staff to task.

"This wasn't a spur-of-the-moment thing. And if Miss Steler was involved, she didn't work alone," he said, and Istvan agreed.

That the bastards could take as much as they had in half an hour and seemingly turn into smoke was amazing. The crown jewels were just the tip of the iceberg, albeit the most important among the artifacts that had disappeared.

"The cameras went out?" he asked. "Don't we have backup?"

"We have an alarm that gets triggered if recording is stopped or if the tape is blank." Miklos's face hardened. "But recording kept going. We have half an hour of footage of Channel Three. Someone hacked into the system from the outside. That's not supposed to be possible."

"And the people whose job it was to watch the monitors?" Arpad asked.

"Killed."

The guards who'd protected the Royal Treasury had been murdered, as well. The mood in the office could not have been more grim.

"How sure are you that Miss Steler was involved?" Janos asked.

"One hundred percent. I showed her the treasury earlier. She begged Chancellor Egon to take her back there, telling him she needed to take more notes and think things over. She charmed him by asking for his help with the selection process." The whole story came out once the Chancellor had calmed down enough to talk. "When the Chancellor had to run off for a quick meeting, she convinced him to leave her locked in there so she could keep working until he returned. He left her with a guard."

"And when he went back, the guards were all dead, and Miss Steler and the loot were missing," Janos finished for him, still wearing a tux. He'd been pulled from a formal reception for the top economists of the nation. Istvan hated social obligations. Janos very much enjoyed that sort of thing.

"Lauryn Steler," Arpad was saying the name pensively, staring at the treasury's blueprint.

He should have seen it coming, Istvan thought. He should have fought harder to keep her from entering the country, or should have put her under heavy guard, or at the very least should have issued a preemptive order to forbid anyone from letting her near the treasury without his being present.

"When we find her, we'll find her team. Who is looking for her?" he asked, gathering his thoughts, pushing back on the regret and the anger. He needed to calm his mind to be able to think more clearly.

"The police and every man I have available. Every border station, airport, train station, bus station and shipping port has her name and picture," Miklos reassured him, but from the resignation in his voice it was clear that he knew how little those precautions meant in reality.

Someone like Lauryn Steler would have multiple passports and could switch between identities with ease. Hell, she could be anywhere by now, traveling as a gray-haired grandmother.

But she had to have left a trail, however faint.

Istvan reached a decision. "I'm going out there. I have contacts."

To break into the palace she had to have local help, and he knew most of the local bad boys in the stolen arts and artifacts world, and had helped to put some of them behind bars one time or another. Anybody hit one of his digs or cherished museums, he went after them with a vengeance. He knew exactly where to look, whom to pressure.

"We're going with you," his brothers said as one, moving closer together.

"A reassuring show of loyalty. Thank you. But it would only complicate things." A few years back, they had resurrected the Brotherhood of the Crown in secret, but in this case he was certain he'd be better off alone. "It'll be difficult enough for me to get out of the palace unnoticed and go around asking questions without attracting media attention."

Arpad looked as if he might argue the point, but then said, "A brief press conference about a security breach should keep the media busy in the press room. Nothing about the loss of the crown jewels, of course." He was always good at seeing the big picture and protecting others. All useful attributes for a Crown Prince.

"We have things on hand for undercover ops. Disguise." Miklos headed for the metal lockers in the back, the staff immediately clearing a path for him.

"I can distract your bodyguard while you leave the palace," Janos offered.

Due to prior attacks on the royal family, at least one

guard had to escort the princes at all times when they left the grounds, a recent royal order by the Queen that drove all of them crazy. They were all rather attached to their independence.

Miklos came back with a box. "While you're scouring the underworld for tips, I'll investigate how they got in and out. I already have a forensics team over at the treasury. Whatever they find should give us some clues to follow."

Janos and Arpad were heading off, clapping Istvan on the shoulder.

"Stay safe," Janos said.

"And bring the crown back," Arpad added. "If we can get everything back in a few days, nobody needs to know what happened. If we can't, we'll deal with it then."

They all agreed on that, given the sharp political climate and their mother's health. The Queen was feeling poorly again. Istvan swore he would solve this latest disaster before news could reach her and put more stress on her system.

His hands fisted at his sides. This wasn't just an attack on the treasury. This was a direct attack on his family and his heritage, the two things most important to him.

"I'll bring back the coronation jewels and see to it that Lauryn Steler pays miserably for taking them," he promised.

NIGHT HAD FALLEN BY the time he found the first usable clue. He'd dealt with thieves in the past and had a network of informants, one of whom came through half an hour earlier. The meeting left a bad taste in Istvan's mouth. Now he owed a favor he knew he was going to hate paying back. But he understood that sometimes he had to compromise on smaller issues to obtain something that was even more important.

The man had heard of something going down at the South Side shipyard tonight. A cousin of his worked there and blabbed about a recent bribe. Istvan had called in the tip and agreed with Miklos that a large-scale search would only draw attention and maybe even allow the thieves to escape in the confusion.

And he wasn't sure if anything would pan out here anyway. For all he knew, this could be some minor drug deal. He didn't want to pull Miklos's men who were doing random vehicle checks on the highways and had as much chance of finding something as he did. But he did accept the five corporate security guards Janos sent from his company.

Hungry and tired, he watched the shipyard, alert for any movement. Hundreds of metal shipping crates were piled in orderly rows, giant cranes towering over them. He was near the loading docks, but with the shipyard lit up, he could see even the dry docks in the distance and the small cruise ship that was currently under repair.

"Six vessels at the loading docks," came the latest intel through his headset.

"We'll split up," he ordered and moved forward to the first in line, a flat-bottomed riverboat.

Since Valtria had no seaport, they used these boats

to take cargo down through Italy to the mouth of the river. The shipping containers were then transferred to much larger ocean liners and made their way to various worldwide destinations from there.

He took the first boat and realized quickly that he'd made a mistake. The containers were all empty, damaged. They were probably going no farther than the factory four miles down the river where they would be recycled. He checked the crew's cabins and the engine house anyway, but found no one and nothing of interest. The boat was completely deserted.

He scratched his nose, his face itching under the disguise Miklos had concocted. At least the sun was below the horizon, so he was no longer sweating.

He sneaked back down the plank and caught sight of a small boat on the water, headed for shore. No lights. The motor wasn't going either, no other sound disturbing the night but the waves gently lapping the docks. The boat drifted, although clearly there was someone at the helm.

Istvan could think of only one reason why the man would want to remain unnoticed. He probably had something to hide. He could have come from the riverboat moored in the middle of the water. It must have been loaded earlier in the day and was still waiting for some permit and the go-ahead, but the captain had been kind enough to leave the loading dock so another vessel could take his place. South Side Port was often crowded.

The captain would get his papers first thing in the morning when the office opened and be off posthaste to wherever he was going. Except, as Istvan watched, the riverboat pulled up anchor and began moving with the current. A quiet departure in the middle of the night.

His instincts prickled even as he realized that every moment he hesitated, the riverboat would only move farther away from him. He jumped without thought, hit the cold water and came up for air, felt his pocketknife slip from his pocket, grabbed after it, but couldn't find it in the dark. Damn. At least he still had his gun. He shoved it tighter into his waistband, then swam as fast as he could, carried by the current, grateful that the man in the boat didn't seem to notice him, hadn't heard the splash.

All the princes were strong swimmers. Soon, he caught up with the impossibly long boat and went around the propellers, then grabbed on to a rope that had been carelessly left to trail the water.

He climbed up with effort, his hands wet and slippery, but eventually he vaulted over the side and ducked down just in time. A handful of men loitered on deck ahead, around an open shipping container. He caught the glint of a rifle, which helped him decide that he'd seen enough to have Port Authority stop and search the ship. Even if the crown jewels weren't on board, something else most certainly was that shouldn't have been.

He reached for his radio to call in the information, settling into a spot where he could remain unseen in the meantime and keep an eye on the container and the men.

But the radio was dead, water dripping from the

earpiece. Same with his cell phone. He should have called before he'd jumped into the river. Miklos would have thought of that. Arpad, too. But they were military. As much time as he spent in the field and even fancied himself an adventurer, Istvan was an academic, not a soldier.

But all was not lost, he thought, when the men were called to the pilot's cabin, leaving the container unlocked and free for him to search the contents. He would have specific information when he swam back to shore to alert Port Authority. Maybe slipping back into the water quietly, right now, would have been the smartest thing, but he couldn't be this close to the royal treasure and not know for sure.

He crept forward, keeping in the shadows, aware that he was leaving a wet trail on deck. The late summer night was warm with a slight breeze. With some luck, his tracks would dry before anyone came this way.

The possibility of a find drew him forward as it had many times in the past. He could hear voices up ahead, but didn't see anyone, and he was too far away to make out what they were saying. He kept an eye out for Lauryn, listened for her voice. If the crown jewels were on the ship, she had to be somewhere around, as well. Someone like her would never let treasure like this too far from her, not until she handed it over to her buyer. He didn't think that had happened yet. The stolen artifact business in Valtria was relatively small-time, thanks to his efforts. The more he thought about it, the more trouble he had picturing any of the known players with enough money to pay for something this big, even at devalued black market prices.

And if the buyer was foreign, Lauryn's fee would include delivering the goods safely to him, smuggling everything neatly out of the country.

Her face and figure floated into his mind unbidden, a mocking smile on her lips and the light of satisfaction in her eyes. She had to be laughing her behind off at how easy it had been to trick them all, to trick *him*. He pressed his lips together as he swore in silence to wipe that smile off her face at the earliest opportunity. The thing to remember was that she was even more dangerous than he'd thought. He wouldn't make the mistake of underestimating her again.

He made his way to the container without trouble, but other than carefully stacked crates, he saw little in the darkness. He pulled the gun, then stepped inside. At least the gun would work. Miklos had assured him that it was the latest and greatest military model and, among other things, water-resistant. Good thing, since he'd forgotten to consider that, too, before jumping in the water.

He tried the first crate. Nailed down. Ten minutes of looking around brought him no luck with the others, so he moved farther in, hoping he would find something to pry those nails loose with.

Nothing.

But he did find an open crate at the very end of the line. And the thirteenth-century war chest inside was more than familiar. His heart beat faster as he ran his fingers over the wood, polished by hundreds of hands through history, some of the paint worn off in places. For the first time since he'd laid eyes on Lauryn Steler, he smiled, because if the men on the ship had one thing from the treasury, then most likely they had the rest of the stolen treasure, as well. The coronation jewels *would* be recovered.

He opened the chest, not expecting to find much, but was rewarded by the sight of Lauryn's notebook and pen, further proof of her involvement. He left them there, trying the next crate but only the one with the war chest had been opened. Still, he was certain now that he had what he'd been looking for right here.

Part of him didn't want to let the crates out of his sight. Another part knew that to save them he had to get help. The sooner he made contact and had the riverboat stopped, the better. He headed out reluctantly, not looking forward to getting back into the night water, but ready to do whatever was required to stop Lauryn and her gang of criminals.

But then two things happened at the same time. He heard—but could not see from behind a stack of crates—men at the door, metal creaking as they worked to seal the container for the journey. And Lauryn Steler stepped out in front of him with something in her hands, cutting him unaware, hitting him on the head so hard that he staggered backward.

After that, he could neither see nor hear.

LAURYN LOOKED OVER THE man's prone body, her heart going a mile a minute. Not that she would let a little adrenaline rush shake her. She'd been in tighter spots than this and had escaped.

Being trapped here didn't scare her nearly as much as the implications of this whole incident. She'd sweated blood over the past couple of years to earn trust in the art industry, to change her reputation. If even a shadow of doubt fell on her regarding this heist, her new career would be over. Her new life as she knew it would cease to exist. She would lose everything.

And Prince Istvan would be the first to crucify her. He wouldn't care if she were guilty or innocent. She'd seen that look in his eyes. If he'd had his way, he would have had her arrested just for thinking of coming near his treasury. He was as judgmental as he was good-looking. Too bad, because she truly respected what he had achieved in his field. He was an amazing archaeologist and practically the patron saint of preservation. But he wouldn't give her the benefit of the doubt.

Nobody would after this.

Once again, she felt the tentacles of her past reach for her, wrap around her and squeeze. She shivered, as if her body was trying to shake them off.

She could see little; not much moonlight filtered in through the small rust holes on top. The man's shape was familiar, but his face wasn't. He had a dark mustache and a nose that looked as if it had been broken at one point. He was no threat to her. She'd taken off his belt and tied him up, gagged him with an oily rag she'd found in a corner.

The bad news was, she was now locked in the damned

container. The good news was, she had at least nailed one of the bastards and had his gun, although she hadn't the faintest idea what to do with it. But if things went badly, he might come in handy as a hostage.

She sat with her back against a crate and waited for him to wake. She didn't have to wait long.

His dark gaze found her and focused on her as soon as his eyes popped open. He struggled against his restraints. She let him. If he wanted to tire himself out, that was fine by her. She didn't worry about the belt giving. She knew a hundred ways to tie a knot, one for every purpose.

"Hmm." He made an unintelligible noise as he glared.

"Stay put and stay quiet," she told him. Then it occurred to her that he could be a source of information. Knowing who these people were and where they were heading might help her better engineer her escape.

Or, if he wasn't with those men, he could tell her who on earth he was. Because now that she thought about it, why would they send one of their own into the container and then lock him in? If they knew that this guy was here, wouldn't they have come looking for him when he didn't return?

She held the gun on him while tugging the gag free from his mouth with her other hand. The threat was implicit.

He understood and didn't shout. "I should have had you barred from the country," he said, enraged but keeping it at a low decibel level.

That voice, those eyes... And her heart about stopped. "Your Highness?" She reached for the mustache on reflex. It came away in her hand. She jerked back, knowing that in some kingdoms, the touching of a royal person without his or her permission was punishable by death. Not that she thought Valtria was that archaic, but truth be told, she wasn't comfortable with touching its hostile prince.

"The nose piece, too," he ordered, then added in a less angry voice, "It itches."

There was her permission. She felt his skin and found the ridge, pulled off an oddly shaped 3D bandage kind of something that blended in perfectly while changing the shape of his nose. Her mind was spinning like a whirligig, but couldn't come up with an explanation for his sudden appearance. "What are you doing here?"

"I could ask the same, but let's not pretend we both don't know the answer to that." He seemed to be choking with barely controlled anger. "This has been your plan all along. You pulled it off. Congratulations."

The accusation felt like a kick in the face. "Right. I plan a good kidnapping at least once a year. To others, it might be cumbersome, but to me, it's like a vacation," she snapped, hating that he would immediately think the worst of her, even if it was exactly what she'd expected.

"If you're not guilty of anything, then there's no reason for you to be scared of me. You can put the gun down and untie me." He struggled to a sitting position, taking over even though he was practically her prisoner.

He was tall and lean, wide-shouldered and dark-eyed like the rest of his brothers. According to the media, he was the least social of the princes, something of an introvert.

Now that they'd met twice, she could certainly see why. Probably nobody could tolerate his paranoia and temper. Too bad. She'd come to the country with nothing but respect for the man and his body of work.

"I'm not scared of you," she told him. Not that he wasn't physically powerful, but she had plenty of moves he hadn't seen yet. "But while I know I'm not guilty, you're too prejudiced and stubborn to believe that. And if you tried something..." He should know that she wasn't going to stand still while he steamrolled over her. "I've worked hard to change my reputation and achieve the standing I have in this business. I wouldn't want to ruin it by shooting a prince."

He swore under his breath in French.

"Hey, I understood that."

He glared. "So why don't you tell me your perfectly innocent version of events." His voice dripped with sarcasm. "Maybe you can convince me."

If only. But it wasn't as if she had anything better to do. A long tale might calm him enough so that she could untie him. She had to do that eventually. He was a prince. Despite what she'd said, she probably wouldn't shoot him. But she couldn't set him free until she could be sure that he wouldn't try to overtake her and tie her up in turn. One of them would get hurt. And because he was a prince, she had a feeling that whatever the outcome of such a struggle would be, it wouldn't be to her advantage.

"After you barely let me take a look at the artifacts in the treasury, I realized you were going to do your best not to let me back in there. I asked the Chancellor, who is a true gentleman by the way, to allow me some more time. I figured that was my only chance to do a thorough job and make sure I made the right choices." The treasury was simply breathtaking, the most amazing place she'd ever seen. She wished—for a multitude of reasons—that they were both still back there.

"How convenient that the Chancellor had to step out," he said with derision.

"Not at all. He was most helpful about the history of some of the objects. And he was very entertaining. A gracious host." Unlike the prince had been, she thought, but left that part unspoken. No sense annoying an already-angry lion, even if he was tied and she had a gun on him.

"Which probably wouldn't have stopped you from murdering him if he didn't have to leave. Are you aware that nine men were killed? Men with wives and children who grieve them. Or were you rushing too fast to count?"

The anger in his voice was like a physical force, overwhelming and real. She thought of the young guard the Chancellor had left with her, and drew a slow breath. The man had pimples, for heaven's sake. Couldn't have been more than early twenties. Now he was dead, and others, as well.

"Fine, so it's not fair that they died and I lived." She pressed her lips together for a second, feeling the guilt, hating the prince for placing more blame on her and adding to the weight. "I was in the enclosure with the carpets and the war chests. We heard a commotion in front of the door. The guard rushed toward it. I thought I heard something that sounded like a gun being fired with a silencer. I slipped into the nearest war chest just as the door opened."

He had the gall to laugh at that. "Oh, an innocent bystander. A victim even. Well done, Miss Steler. You're a very creative woman. If my hands were free, I would clap."

Keep it up and we'll never be free. "Fine. Think what you will." She stood and walked away from him.

"Thank you," he called after her, as arrogant and full of himself as ever. "I think I'll do that."

She checked the door. Locked, just as she'd suspected. If she had her old tools, it wouldn't have posed a problem, but she had nothing with her save a pen and a notebook that she'd left on the bottom of the chest in which she'd hidden. She'd figured whoever was breaking in would go for gold. How was she to know that they would take the war chest, too?

She walked back to Istvan. "Where are we exactly?"

"On a ship called *Valtrian Freedom*, heading south, not that you don't know that better than I do. Out of curiosity, who is your buyer?"

She shoved the gun in the back of her pants so she

could put her hands on her hips. She simply watched him for a while, trying to decide whether reasoning with him would be a waste of breath. It would be. But she found she couldn't help herself.

"First, I don't steal. Second, even if I did, I'd never be stupid enough to steal crown jewels. Not very low-profile, is it? And not marketable either. They're easily recognizable. As stolen artifacts, they'd be completely useless. The safest way would be selling the stones separately and melting down the gold, but that's such a small fraction of their value. And a good thief could easily steal gold and gems from a number of other sources with a lot less difficulty."

He stared at her without a response. Apparently, her words had given him something to think about. Not long enough. "Maybe it doesn't make sense, but it doesn't have to," he said after a while. "It could have been a crime of passion. You saw the coronation jewels and you couldn't resist them."

She shook her head. "You know it as well as I do that this wasn't a spur-of-the-moment thing. This was a carefully planned and meticulously executed heist. There are not that many people in the world who have crews that can pull off something like this. And I'm not one of them."

"No longer one of them?" he pushed. "Or are the rumors true and you always worked alone?"

She said nothing to that. She never discussed her past.

"You know these crews?"

Again, she remained silent.

"If you didn't do this, do you have any idea who did?"

She shook her head.

She'd thought about little else while she'd been hiding in the chest. She had plenty of time on the way over here, then while she waited for the men to walk away from the container. Then she finally opened the top, busted the crate's lid and climbed out. The container door had still been open. But she hesitated too long between escaping and staying with the royal treasures.

Then someone came in, and she thought it was one of the thieves, about to discover her. So she'd done what she had to. But while she was busy with him, the door had been sealed and she'd lost the option of leaving.

"Could you untie the belt? You may keep the gun," he said.

"Aren't you the magnanimous one? You're in no position to negotiate," she reminded him, but untied him anyway. He was considering other options at least and didn't look as if he would attack her on the spot.

He rubbed his hands over his wrists, closed his eyes for a second, and for a moment looked almost vulnerable. Must have been a trick of the shadows.

"Are you okay?" she asked anyway before she could stop herself. She did hit him over the head pretty hard back there.

His fierce frown was an immediate rebuke. "Fine."

"Let me look at you." She leaned forward to check

his irises, chancing that he might grab for the gun, but couldn't see much in the dark.

He drew back as if offended. "That's not necessary."

"Do you have any nausea? I could have given you a concussion." Considering the way he'd been treating her, she felt only mildly guilty.

"You didn't."

"You don't know that. Anyway, if you feel sleepy, try to stay awake."

"I do not have a concussion," he said, stiff-lipped.

His obstinacy was ticking her off on every level. "You're too tough to get a concussion from a girl, is that it?"

He came to his feet and strode away from her, stopped as far as the crate allowed, then stared back. An image of buffalo came into her mind, pawing the snow, blowing steam out of his nose. No need to share that with him.

She gave him a minute before she followed. "How far is the nearest seaport?"

"Trieste would be two hours at the most."

She considered options and backup options, trying to come up with an escape plan. "What do you think will happen when we get there?"

"If we're lucky, they'll open the container to transfer the stolen goods. That'll give us a chance to make a break for it."

"I don't believe in luck." She peered through the darkness and tried to map the place.

The prince gave a brief nod. “Me neither.”

So for two hours they searched every corner, tried to find a weak spot where they could break out—there wasn’t one—and made plans on what they’d do once the riverboat reached port and the container would be opened.

Except that it wasn’t.

No sooner did the boat stop moving than they felt the container lift as a crane hoisted it in the air. She slid against the prince who in turn slid against the back wall, then shifted quickly to the side, saving them from being crushed to death by some unstable crates.

He wedged himself into the corner and held off what had to be a couple of hundred pounds with his bare hands. Then the container settled with a loud clunk and everything stopped moving.

“I take it this would be the ocean liner,” she said, a little rattled, which annoyed her. She didn’t like thinking that the prince might have just saved her. She prided herself on being a self-sufficient woman. She didn’t want to owe anything to any stuck-up, prejudiced Valtrian royalty.

She handed his gun back to him, a kind of payback, she supposed.

“I’m not too keen on going on an ocean voyage at the moment.” Prince Istvan strode to the front and pointed at the lock from the inside. “Are you sure you can’t open this?”

“Not with my bare hands.” That was as close to admitting her shady past as she was comfortable with.

"I have a tool for you." He pointed the mean-looking handgun in the general direction. "Show me where to shoot."

"It'll be too loud."

"Not if I shoot just as they rattle the next container into place."

She felt around in the near darkness, then grabbed the barrel of the gun and pressed it against the right spot. "Here."

He aimed. They waited. Then when they could hear chains creak and the corner of the next container bump against another, he squeezed off a shot. Inside the container, the sound seemed deafening. But she had a feeling that with all the machinery and the noise of the harbor outside, it had been barely noticeable. Still, they waited a few minutes. When no one raised the alarm and no one came to investigate, the prince drew back, then slammed his shoulder into the door before she could stop him.

That had to hurt. She winced.

"Patience." She stepped over to examine the damage to the lock. "You'll need at least one more shot."

Except that the crane seemed to move on to the other side of the ship. He waited on the spot anyway, in case the crane came back. It didn't. An hour or so later they felt the ship shudder, the engines start and the ground move under their feet. Istvan used that distraction to fire off his second shot, which did the trick at last.

This time when he shoved his shoulder into the door, it opened.

Four inches.

Just enough for them to see that they were blocked in by another container in front of them.

"Trapped." She closed her eyes for a moment against the disappointment and frustration. She could have banged her head against the metal. They should have done something much sooner, on the riverboat. But the prince had thoroughly distracted her, and now it was too late. The very reason she always worked alone. A partner was nothing but trouble.

"Going in an unknown direction on a strange ship," he thought out loud. His voice sounded off.

"A ship that's controlled by criminals." Not that she blamed all this on him. Maybe a little. If he'd let her do her work in the treasury earlier, she would have been done and gone by the time the thieves got there. He would have still suspected her, but she could have been dealing with that unfair cloud of suspicion at the five-star hotel where the Getty was putting her up, instead of here.

"Or your friends. Although, the two might not be mutually exclusive, I suspect." Apparently, he still harbored some mistrust of her.

"People we don't want to meet up with," she offered as compromise. "At this point, if they found us, they'd kill both of us. They sure didn't hesitate shooting the guards at the treasury." The memory turned her mood even more somber. "And they *will* find us. If not sooner, then when they come to get the loot."

The more she thought of that, the bigger that lead ball grew in her stomach.

And bigger yet when he said, "Just so we're clear, I still think that you're involved in this in some way. And when we get out of here and I return the crown jewels to the treasury, I *will* figure out what your role has been. And then I'll personally see to it that you're prosecuted to the full extent of Valtrian law, Miss Steler."

Chapter Three

His stomach rolled with each wave that the ship encountered and there was an endless supply of those. When he went on longer trips, he usually took a pill to counter his motion sickness. There'd be no relief here.

Istvan leaned back against a crate as he sat on the ground, his arms resting on his pulled-up knees. He was passing the time by mentally listing his theories about Lauryn. Either she was in the container because she stole the treasure and wanted to stay as close to it as possible. Or because she'd stolen the treasure and then had a falling-out with her partners who locked her in. Or she'd witnessed the treasure being stolen while she was looking for pieces for the Getty, the heist got her blood heated and she followed the treasure, thinking she could take it from the thieves and keep it for herself. He didn't give much credit to her claims of being completely innocent.

"Are you sure you don't have a concussion?" she asked him, sitting opposite.

He resented her concern, given that it was more than

likely that she had something to do with their current circumstances. “Quite certain.”

That only kept her quiet for a minute.

“We have no food or water,” she said, stating the obvious.

“A good thing, because we don’t have a toilet either,” he said just to torture her.

She pursed her lips as she stood. “That’s it, then. I’m getting out of here.”

She did have an indomitable spirit, he had to give her that. “How?”

“I’m going to think of something.”

“Happy thoughts will give you wings?” he mocked her.

“You can’t underestimate the power of positive thinking.”

Or the power of self-delusion, he thought, hoping she wouldn’t get going and give him a motivational seminar.

She was staring straight up, as if expecting inspiration to drop from heaven. “How many more bullets do you have left?” she asked after a few minutes.

Great, here came the brilliant idea. He checked his gun, not keen on handing it back to her. “Ten.”

“Do you have any matches?”

“How about a lighter?” He didn’t smoke, but he always carried one, along with a pocketknife. Now and then they came in handy at a dig.

“Can I have it with five of the bullets?”

“What for?”

"There's light coming in. Which means rust spots in the top of the container. Weakness. A small explosion could peel back enough for us to squeeze through." She eyed the crates.

He didn't think she was kidding. "You can build a bomb?"

She didn't respond, only held out her hand, as good as an admission—of her bomb-making skills and her past.

After thinking it over and realizing they had few other options, he counted out five bullets for her. "You might see why I was reluctant to put you in charge of a traveling exhibit of Valtrian treasures."

She closed her fingers around the bullets and the lighter. "The skills I have might yet save your treasures."

He couldn't argue with that, so he said nothing. He simply watched as she scaled the crates, a sleek shadow moving swiftly, higher and higher until she disappeared on top. He pulled his dropped chin back into place.

"Do you need help?" he asked belatedly. He wanted out of here and she seemed to want the same thing. Whatever hidden agenda she had, for now it looked as if they were working toward the same goal. They might as well work together. "I can help."

Now and then the setting of charges was necessary at an excavation, although, due to the high risk of damage, he employed that tool as rarely as possible and always had an expert handle it. But he wasn't uncomfortable around explosives.

"Stay covered in case there's flying shrapnel," she called down from her perch.

Shards of steel flying from the top of the container, he realized, were a definite possibility. He looked at the crates. The wood boards were thick enough to protect the contents, his first concern. "And you?" he asked as an afterthought.

"I'll deal."

He started forward. "Look, I—"

A small explosion cut him off, which did send some shrapnel flying and shook the tower of crates Lauryn had climbed.

"Are you okay?" he called up as the dust settled.

"Of course I am."

"They had to have heard that." He put his disguise back on, hoping he got the mustache straight. His swim over to the riverboat had washed off some of the glue. He'd have to be careful not to lose the damn thing completely.

"There're plenty of other noise with all engines going full-steam. And even if they heard us, it'll take them a while to figure out where the noise came from. They might think it was just two containers sliding against each other." She peeked down at him. "The way is clear. Whenever you're ready."

He wasn't one of those super-macho types, but the fact that *she* would be rescuing *him* rubbed him the wrong way. His masculine pride prickled as he climbed the crates. They swayed the whole time, which didn't help his motion sickness.

She was already halfway through the hole when he got there, her shapely behind dangling practically in front of his face. “Watch the edges. They’re pretty sharp.” She grunted. “I could use a hand here.”

For a moment he hesitated, not sure where or how to touch her. He ended up bracing her thighs, which seemed to do the trick. Her muscles flexed against his palms. He ignored the way that made him feel.

She hoisted herself up at last. “Come on.”

He tried. There wasn’t enough room for his shoulders. But he was good at navigating tight spots. He’d spent a lot of time in underground funeral chambers, squeezing through impossible passageways. He twisted, angling one shoulder up, and turning the right way to be able to clear the hole without losing too much skin.

The cool night air felt like heaven on his face.

He sat next to the hole and drew a couple of deep breaths, hoping to steady his stomach. She was already moving along, going for even higher ground, easily climbing the side of another container. He went after her, only succeeding with effort even though he had the advantage of upper-body strength.

She was looking all around when he caught up with her. “Any idea where we are? I can’t see the lights of the land.”

Neither could he, which meant that swimming to shore now was out of the question. He looked up at the sky to get his bearings. “Heading southeast for now.” Of course, that was pretty much a given. They had to get out of the Adriatic. “Once we reach the Mediterranean

Sea, we'll see if the ship is heading toward Asia, Africa or for the Atlantic."

"How soon will we know?"

"In a couple of hours." They were traveling at a good clip.

"Any idea what we could do in the meanwhile?"

He looked out over the vast rows of containers and could make out the bridge up front. He drew a deep breath. "We could try taking over the ship."

HER IDEAS HAD BEEN more along the line of jumping ship and swimming for shore, but she could see the white froth of the waves in the moonlight. The water was too rough, the mainland too far away.

"Look." She pointed toward the starboard side.

A half-dozen men were walking the ship with flashlights.

"Maybe they heard the explosion," Istvan observed.

"Or it's a routine check. To make sure the containers are all steady and well-secured. They'd want to know that before the ship goes out to the ocean."

The muscles in his cheeks seemed to tighten as she said *ocean.* And she noticed how tightly he was hanging on to the edge of the container as the whole ship swayed.

Several pieces fell into place. "Are you seasick?"

"Certainly not," he said with heat, which told her she'd hit a nerve.

She sat back on her heels as she examined him. She didn't picture him having any weaknesses. He'd been nothing less than formidable from the moment they'd met. She couldn't help a relieved smile.

"I'm always glad when I can use my misery to entertain others," he groused.

"Having weaknesses makes a person more approachable. You can be harsh, you know." She paused. "You probably do. You probably do it on purpose. I wasn't looking forward to working with you, to be honest."

He pulled up an eyebrow. "The feeling is completely mutual."

She smiled again, at his unflinching honesty, the first thing she liked about the prince.

"Do you always take so much delight in other people's misfortune?" he asked in a wry tone.

"Sorry." She reached back and unhooked her necklace, pulled the round eye hook off with her teeth, rolled off all the pearls save two. She stashed the free pearls in her pocket, then with four knots she secured the remaining two about three finger widths apart. "Give me your wrist."

"I don't wear jewelry."

"Please, you're royalty."

"I wear some symbols of the monarchy on ceremonial occasions," he corrected.

She held his gaze.

"I don't have a problem."

"This will help the problem you don't have."

After a moment of glaring at her, he held out his left hand. She fastened the string so the pearls would be on the inside of his wrist, pressing against the nerves there.

"What is this?" He examined her concoction dubiously, while she made a matching one for his other wrist.

"An acupressure bracelet. My father used to be seasick. He was terrible. You've never seen that shade of purple. He looked like a walking Monet painting when it hit him bad."

The darkening of his face told her that bringing up her father might have been a mistake. "He was a good man, in his own way," she added, feeling the need to defend the man who'd kept her fed and clothed, alive for the first part of her life.

He remained stoic. "Forgive me if I don't take your word for it."

After a moment of silence, he climbed from the top of the container onto the top of the row below them, then down several more levels to the deck. He strode forward between the rows, going pretty fast, pulling into cover each time he reached a gap between two containers.

He was probably trying to make sure the men who were checking the load didn't see him, she thought and copied him. Then they reached the last row and there was nothing but empty deck in front of them and the bridge about a hundred feet away.

He waited and watched.

"What are we looking for?" she asked from behind him.

"I want to know how many men are on this ship and

if they're all armed. Some of these ocean liners work with skeleton crews. Everything's computerized these days."

"That the men at the treasury could take out all those guards means they must have been armed to the teeth."

"Those men might not be here. They could have a connection in shipping who agreed to smuggle the goods out of the country. There could be only a handful of bad apples on this ship, the rest of the crew and the captain honest men. In which case, we can ask for their help. Maybe taking over the ship isn't our only option. It could be as easy as capturing and immobilizing a couple of bad guys."

He was talking as if he believed her innocence at last, but she noticed that he made a point of not turning his back to her. Still, at least he was willing to work with her. They could sort out the rest once they escaped. At least they were no longer locked in. She was feeling more optimistic by the minute.

But their hopes seemed unjustified when, a few seconds later, the patrolling seamen came into view, armed. Every last one of them.

She held her breath and pulled close to Istvan, the two of them sandwiched together in a small gap between two containers, her breasts pressed against his back as she peeked over his shoulder. This was the closest they'd been to each other, and she was suddenly aware of his well-built body, his wide shoulders, the strength of the man as he stood in front of her.

He had his gun in his hand, his other hand holding her back, his feet slightly apart. His body language couldn't have been clearer. If anyone wanted to get to her, they had to go through him. A strange feeling seeped through her, part indignation that he would assume she needed protection, part something else.

She wasn't used to feeling protected by men.

She'd certainly never been protected by her father who'd used her even as a small child as his "little helper" in his often dangerous business. Sure, she'd been sheltered and fed, but she'd had to earn that food and the roof over her head.

The men kept walking, talking too low for her to understand. She had half a mind to elbow her way in front of the prince, or at least right next to him, but the fact was, he had a gun and she didn't. And while she was a self-sufficient and independent woman, she was also smart enough to correctly assess the situation they were in.

"This way," Istvan said and moved to the right between the first row of containers and the second once the men passed.

They were hidden from view of the bridge, moving away from the men who were checking the deck. Regardless, he stole forward with caution.

And still neither of them saw the guy who'd been hiding between the containers until it was too late. He was seated, a bottle of booze in one hand, an AK-47 in the other. He immediately lifted the rifle.

Istvan jumped forward, knocking the rifle to the left

while pressing his own weapon against the man's chest and pulling the trigger. The body had muffled the sound, but it was still unmistakable.

"Come on." Istvan tossed the dead man's rifle to her, then ran, probably in case anyone had been close enough to hear the muffled shot and was coming to investigate.

The whole incident lasted less than thirty seconds, Lauryn thought bewildered, running after him, her heart still banging desperately against her chest. Violence always shook her. Even back when she'd made her living in ways less than one-hundred-percent honest, she never took a weapon to a heist, prided herself on being able to get in and out unseen, unconfronted.

The prince had been quick in a crisis situation, acted without hesitation, done well. Maybe too well, she realized suddenly, for a prince.

"Where did you learn all the cloak-and-dagger stuff?" she asked as they slowed.

"Basic self-defense training all the princes received."

She nearly laughed. "I wouldn't buy that at a two-for-the-price-of-one sale. Want to try again?"

"A couple of years ago, I led an expedition to the Middle East. I was searching for the remains of a caravan a Valtrian king sent to the Far East a few centuries ago. The whole caravan had perished. I was trying to find some trace of it and figure out what happened to them, but my crew and I ended up stumbling into the middle of some serious tribal warfare."

She looked at him and felt her lips stretch into a shaky smile.

"What is it?"

"You live a more interesting life than I gave you credit for."

He flashed a smile back, the first he'd ever given her. It transformed his face in the moonlight from handsome to dazzling, and she had to catch her breath.

She'd thought of him as a soft academic before who'd been bitten by the archaeology bug. Sure, he published a lot, but she always thought someone else did the lion's share of the fieldwork. She couldn't picture a prince with a shovel and a wheelbarrow, getting his hands dirty. But suddenly it looked as if there was more to him than being a high-born professor. Those princely manners hid a warrior spirit.

She couldn't say she wasn't fascinated by it.

"This changes everything," he said.

She blinked, afraid for a moment that he could read her thoughts. "What does?"

"The man I shot back there. He will be missed. A thorough search of the ship will be conducted."

"Maybe he was a stowaway."

"He was a member of the crew, sneaking off for a drink."

"Why? Those guys looked like nothing more than thugs. I doubt they'd frown on a little whiskey."

"Maybe he was Muslim, forbidden to drink. He can't very well do it in front of the captain or he'd be punished." He cheered up. "If the crew is Muslim, it could mean we're heading to one of the Muslim countries in the region."

"And why is that good?"

"We'll be there by morning."

As opposed to being stuck on the ship for days for a cross-Atlantic voyage to South America or the United States. She was beginning to see his point.

Hopefully, the rest of the crew wouldn't notice that one man missing until then. In the chaos of landing and unloading, the prince and she might be able to slip off the ship unseen and alert the authorities.

Not that life had ever been that easy for her, she reflected the next second as they came around the corner and ran right into the armed posse that was patrolling the deck.

Chapter Four

"Why are you on my ship?" the captain was yelling at them in Turkish, waving the gun his crew had gotten off Istvan. His eyebrows were like fat, hairy caterpillars, wiggling with each word on a face that was lined by age and weather. He had a thick nose and a blunt chin he thrust out as he narrowed one eye. "Are you spies? Are you police?"

They were on the bridge where the instrument panels took up most of the space. The open sea was visible through a bank of windows, stretching endlessly toward the horizon.

"Stowaways," Istvan responded in the man's own language, glancing at Lauryn, who probably didn't understand any of the conversation and was scared to death.

Not that she showed it. On the surface she looked as if she was holding up, which was good. He'd found that in situations like this, the key was not to show fear.

"Where did you come from?" Only the captain was asking questions. The rest of the officers worked the instruments. The posse that captured Istvan and Lauryn contended themselves with pointing their guns and looking menacing.

Istvan kept his gaze on the captain, ignoring the half-dozen weapons. "Valtria."

"Stowaways from Valtria." A bushy eyebrow went up. "I ask you again, what are you doing on my ship?"

The fact that this crew was armed, too, like the one on the riverboat had been, didn't necessarily mean they were criminals. A lot of ocean liner crews armed themselves these days in response to the increasing pirate attacks off the coast of Africa. But the interaction between the captain and the crew said they were hiding something. And the captain was angrier than he should have been at a couple of stowaways. His small, calculating eyes kept returning to Lauryn and not in a good way.

"We're running from the law," Istvan said to distract him. If the man was doing shady business himself, he might sympathize.

"Why?" The captain pointed the gun straight at Istvan, his full attention back on him.

Istvan gave a small nod to Lauryn to reassure her, wishing she could understand what was going on, then put his hands up in a capitulating gesture. Now that he'd seen the crew and how well-armed they were, he had to accept that his plan of taking over the ship had been overly optimistic.

"You're a rich man. No criminal." The captain's eyes narrowed.

And Istvan caught his mistake at once. Raising his

arms caused his shirtsleeve to fall back and reveal his gold watch. Getting caught lying could be the worst thing at the moment.

The man cocked the gun. He didn't look as if he was giving them another chance to explain.

But Lauryn rushed forth with an explanation anyway. "We only pretend to be rich. We're thieves," she said in near-perfect, unaccented Turkish.

Istvan stared at her. The woman was full of surprises. Definitely not one to be underestimated.

"When I was young, in my country thieves got their hands cut off." The captain's scowl deepened, but at least he wasn't shooting. He was measuring up Lauryn.

Istvan used the distraction and eyed the man on his right. He might be able to lunge for the man's rifle. He shifted his weight, getting ready.

"Lucky for us, you're not a policeman." Lauryn smiled with a hint of teasing.

The captain smiled back and Istvan did a double take.

"I wouldn't go as far as to say that you're lucky." He swept his gaze over her from head to toe. "You don't look like a thief."

"Let me reach into my clothes and I'll prove it to you," she challenged him.

Armed men stood behind them, their guns pointed and ready to shoot. The captain nodded to the goon behind Lauryn and the man moved his rifle barrel forward so that it would touch the back of her head.

She rolled her slim shoulders for a brief second before

she reached into her waistband and brought out a pocketknife, tossing it onto the floor at the captain's feet.

"That's mine!" One of the armed men stepped forward, flashing her a dark look.

A watch came next from her bra, similarly claimed. Then some pocket change of Turkish currency from her socks, a lighter from her shoe, a blue medal of the evil eye—a common charm in the Middle East. By the time she tossed a small black book on top of the heap, the men looked ready to strangle her, but the captain was laughing, the lines around his small eyes crinkling with mirth.

"And he's a thief, too?" The man pointed at Istvan with the gun that he'd relaxed during the performance.

Istvan's muscles stiffened. Now they would expect him to put on a show like she had. Brilliant. Because, of course, he had absolutely nothing.

But Lauryn said, "Mostly I'm the thief and he's the muscle."

The man nodded at that, looking Istvan over one more time, his gaze settling on his left wrist. "The watch?"

"An excellent fake." He pulled it off immediately and held it out, an offering.

One of the men snatched it out of his hand and the expensive timepiece immediately disappeared.

Istvan didn't care about the watch. He kept stealing glances at Lauryn. When on earth did she have time to pick these men's pockets anyway? Their struggle when they'd been apprehended had been brief, had been kept brief purposely by Istvan because he didn't want her to get hurt.

The captain shoved the handgun into his waistband, a calculating expression coming to his face as he glanced from one stowaway to the other. "Maybe we'll be friends, eh?"

The rest of the men still had their weapons aimed. They weren't as amused by Lauryn's party tricks as their captain.

The man assessed the prisoners for another few seconds, then seemed to come to a decision when he turned away from them, looking out to sea. "Take them to one of the aft storage cabins. I'll deal with them when we reach Mersin."

The crew grabbed them and didn't worry much about bruising. They were shoved forward, taken down narrow hallways and stairs, a rifle barrel stuck between Istvan's ribs to guide him to their destination. He took note of every turn, the location of every door.

Then they were stopped and he was thrust forward into a small cabin. Lauryn came next, pushed with enough force to lose her balance. He caught her before she would have crashed into the metal shelving that nearly filled out their makeshift prison cell. She felt fragile in his arms, although he knew she was anything but a lost little lamb. He'd seen her in action.

The door closed and locked behind them before they could have turned and tried any trick for getting out of there. She stepped away without looking at him, brushed her clothes off and took a minute to survey the place. "Welcome to the presidential suite," she said in a wry tone.

Hardly. The storage cabin was barely three meters by three meters with a single porthole, which was their only source of light. The switch for the metal-mesh-protected bulb overhead was outside the door and the men hadn't cared enough to turn it on for their prisoners.

His stomach growled. He ignored it. He had a feeling it'd be a long time before any food came their way. Lauryn didn't exactly steal herself into the men's hearts when she'd picked their pockets.

Her performance was more than confirmation enough that at least some of the things rumored about her had to be true. But because her "skill" saved their lives, he couldn't very well hold that against her just now.

"You speak very good Turkish." He checked the shelves, but found nothing beyond spare parts for the ship's machinery.

"I traveled a lot with my father when I was younger."

Her father the tomb raider, lest he forgot. And he couldn't afford to forget where she'd come from and who she was for a second. She might have saved their lives back on the bridge, but they weren't partners. She might have clever words and clever fingers, but he couldn't trust her. "Did he teach you pickpocketing, as well?"

"I don't know what you're talking about," she said bland-faced.

And he felt the corner of his lips tug up at her bravado. He immediately schooled his features back into place. He was willing to accept that they were going to have to work together to get out of this mess, but he was *not* going to enjoy it. And he most definitely was *not* going to like her, under any circumstances.

He turned his attention to the porthole and fiddled with the latch. Locked. Because he'd already looked the shelves over, the points of interest in the room seemed pretty much exhausted. At least in the shipping container he'd been near his precious artifacts and had room to walk around, stretch his legs. Their grand escape so far was turning out to be anything but, taking them from bad to worse.

"Any ideas on how we could get out of here?" Having to ask for advice from her galled him to no end, but there it was. He'd seen enough by now not to underestimate her.

She smirked at him. "I didn't give back everything I took." The smirk turned into a full-blown smile as she pulled a fork from her pocket.

That was it? "I was hoping for a semiautomatic and a set of keys."

"Those who can't value the small things in life, don't deserve the big ones." The smile turned into a look of annoyance. Then her eyebrows went up as she caught him looking at her mouth.

Oh, hell. He focused on the damned fork. "Where did you get that from?"

"Found it on a tray on a side instrument panel. When we were on the bridge. Probably came with the captain's lunch." She examined the lock on the porthole. "What do we do once this thing is open?"

"See if there's a way up to the main deck. Maybe we could get our hands on a lifeboat and slip away before the sun comes up. Why did you take all that stuff anyway?"

"You never know what'll come in handy in an emergency. Anyway, there was no time to evaluate. I grabbed anything I could feel."

He shook his head.

The locking mechanism was nothing more than a hole, must have worked with some kind of a tool. She had to break off two of the fork's tines and bend the other two together to make it work. Her competence was impressive, even if it was competence learned from a profession he disapproved of.

Having the lock popped, however, didn't mean that they were home free. The porthole had been painted over and over again with thick white maritime paint and had stuck shut years ago from the looks of it. She went at it with the mutilated fork. He found a chunk of scrap metal under one of the shelves and helped. Even with the two of them working side by side, it took nearly an hour to set the window free.

But only the smallest metal circle that held the glass in the middle opened. The rest was apparently framing. He stepped back in disappointment. All that time and effort wasted.

She stuck her head out. "This might be beyond your considerable contortionist skills."

He tried anyway, once she stepped aside, not ready to give up yet. Other than a bruised shoulder, he got little for his efforts. And the window had been their only chance. The door didn't have a lock on the inside, nothing to pick. And this time he didn't have a weapon to shoot the lock apart.

He sat on the floor and braced his back against the shelving, cataloging the contents of the small space, trying to think of anything he could use to break out of the place. There had to be a way.

Lauryn hung her upper body out the porthole again to get a good look up. Then she looked to the front. "I think I see something on the horizon ahead of the ship."

He ignored the tempting curve of her hips that was framed by the window. "Probably another ship. Fifteen percent of all the world's shipping goes through here."

"Can we signal to them?"

"Not from this far." Although, the idea held merit. "If they come closer."

He wore a black sports jacket he could wave from the window. Lauryn had on a black shirt. He would have preferred her to be the one to undress for rescue's sake, frankly. With her leaning out and her shapely behind dangling practically in arm's reach, he was beginning to become aware of her as more than a possibly reformed thief. She blocked most of the light, but his brain was happy to supply details he couldn't see. Nothing had ever been wrong with his imagination, unfortunately.

"We need something white. Black won't stand out

against the ship's black side, especially in the darkness," she said, her mind on more practically issues.

Too bad he'd chosen a dark blue shirt to wear that morning.

"It's not a ship," she said after a while. "It's bigger."

"Could be one of the Greek islands. There are more than two hundred of them." Janos often went there yachting. He wished he had his brothers with him or that, at least, they knew where he was. There was no trouble the six of them couldn't manage together.

"I think I see lights."

That had potential. "About forty of the islands are inhabited."

She slipped back in. "I can fit through the porthole. If the ship sails closer to the island, I'll swim to shore and get help." Her voice brimmed with excitement.

He had a feeling her face would be lit up, too, if he could only see it. But with their only source of light outside, her features were shadowed.

"No."

"I'm a strong swimmer."

"No." To emphasize his point, he went to the window and sat on the floor right beneath it. The fresh air eased his seasickness and if she dived for the porthole to escape him, he could catch her.

"You don't trust me," she accused him after a minute, her initial excitement waning. "You don't think I'd send help."

He watched her for a while before he responded. "The

thought did cross my mind." Her criminal background didn't exactly spell *trustworthy.*

Because she'd turned to him, the moonlight was in her face. She looked as if she was ready to murder him. His gaze dropped to the fork, still in her hand. Looked like the perfect tool for skewering any number of body parts he'd be reluctant to sacrifice. He pulled up his knees.

"Of all the pigheaded—" She stepped to the left, then to the right, using up all the room available for pacing. "If you let me go, I might or might not bring help. If you don't, you're not going to get help, guaranteed. Isn't at least getting a chance worth the risk?"

"Not from where I'm sitting." Just because she didn't seem to be in league with the captain, it didn't mean she wasn't involved in the heist. She could have been part of the retrieval crew, while the captain was transport. They could be working for the same person without knowing about one another. She could have been locked in the container by accident, or on purpose, to guard the treasures until final delivery.

All right, so she'd helped them escape the container, and she'd helped to avoid immediate execution by the ship's captain, but Istvan still wasn't about to let her go until he was sure about her and had a crystal-clear picture of her involvement in the theft of the Valtrian crown jewels.

"So I'm what, your prisoner?" She huffed, her hands on her hips, a stance that only accentuated her exceptional figure, which could have been a conscious, distracting maneuver on her part.

He refused to be distracted. "More like a cellmate. We're both prisoners here."

"But I could escape! And help you," she added quickly.

"Too dangerous. The currents are pretty strong. And the ship won't go close to any of the smaller Greek islands. It'll stay in deep water. It'll go close to shore only if it's headed for harbor, and none of the small islands down here have a harbor large enough to accommodate a ship this size."

"I could try."

He was done explaining. She wasn't going anywhere. The end.

She sat down, her back against the door, and glared at him. "I can't believe I'm being kidnapped by a prince. There should be a code of honor, you'd think, with royalty."

He fought a sudden grin. Under different circumstances, he might have appreciated the fire in her, although, hitherto he hadn't been aware that he liked fire in a woman. Amalia had always been soft-spoken and accommodating. "Consider it more like protective custody."

She stuck her chin out. She had a pretty chin, delicately shaped like the rest of her. Her tumultuous eyes narrowed. "I could take you."

"Your trying would certainly make our journey more

interesting." He wouldn't have minded it a bit, provided that she put that cursed fork down already.

Her lips tightened. So did her fist around the fork.

He drew a deep breath, appreciating the cool night breeze that came through the porthole, helping his stomach to remain semi-settled. *The porthole...*

"You're looking at me funny," she was saying.

He stood as the puzzle pieces came together in his head and a plan gelled. "We need a place to hide."

"Ha!"

All right, he got her point. The storage room was insanely small, every corner instantly visible from the door even with the half-empty storage shelves. But there was Turkish writing and some symbols on one wall. He moved there and ran his finger over the metal sheeting until he found a screw head. "I think there might be an electric panel back here. Would you hand me that fork?"

She did so grudgingly.

The edge was too blunt, of course. He had to work it on the rough steel of the floor to sharpen it. He got the first screw out, then the next and another. Having to work by nothing but moonlight didn't make his job easier, nor did the rust. But finally he was able to lift the panel off and take a look at the jumble of electric cables that ran beneath it.

"What's this?" Lauryn asked from behind him.

"Room to hide." He pushed aside the cables and was able to create a small nook. *Room for one.* He looked around, his gaze settling on two cardboard boxes on a bottom shelf, and his decision was made. "You squeeze in here."

"Not a chance." She took a step back, as if to emphasize her words. She folded her arms in front of her, her shoulders stiffening.

"You're smaller than I am."

She eyed the hole warily. "Say I do get in there. Then what? I have no way to hold the panel in place from the inside."

He took a thorough look at the smooth metal. "I'll put the screws back in."

"You want to wall me up? I better touch up my makeup. Something must have smeared and made me look stupid."

She looked anything but, with her fine eyes throwing sparks as she faced him.

"This is what I'm thinking," he said, tamping down his untimely masculine appreciation. "We leave the porthole open. When they come to give us food or water or to get us for more questioning, they'll find the place empty. They'll think we jumped."

She considered him. "And because we've flown the coop, so to speak, there won't be a reason to lock the door when they go to report to the captain."

He liked her quick wit. "Exactly."

Her eyes narrowed. "How about if I wall you in?"

Did everything have to be a battle with her? "I wouldn't fit."

"I don't like electricity."

"It gives heat and light, what's not to like?" He was never going to understand women.

"I got shocked as a kid."

That explained things. "You won't get shocked now. Look, it's all completely insulated. Just stay still."

"And if you leave me behind?"

"You have to trust me."

"Like you trusted me to swim for help?"

He rubbed his nape for a second. "It's different."

"Because you're a prince and you think you can order me around." Her hands went to her hips again as she glared at him.

He wanted to kiss her. Utter nonsense. The swaying of the ship was scrambling his brain.

"That, too," he admitted. "Plus, I have the fork. And I'm not afraid to use it." Maybe some humor would disarm her.

A smile hovered above her top lip. Then she said, "I want it to be noted that I'm trusting you, even though you were completely unwilling to trust me."

Not entirely fair, to be certain. "Might I point out that between the two of us I'm not the one with a history of criminal activity?"

"I have no idea what you're talking about. I wish you would stop insinuating things," she told him.

He motioned toward the crevice, pitying every policeman who'd ever had to interrogate her. "Are you going to get in there before someone comes or would you like to wait and chat a little longer?"

She drew a deep breath and did an about-face. "Let

me see this." She arranged a few more wires, turned again and stepped in backward. Flattened herself. "And where will you be?"

"Leave that to me." He picked up the panel.

"Watch my nose," she snapped at him.

Unnecessarily. He was already watching the parts of her that stuck out. Mostly her breasts, but they stuck out farther than her nose anyway.

His gaze traveled up and met hers. She looked miserable. He couldn't blame her. On a rare impulse, he leaned forward and pressed a brief kiss on her lips, then gently put the panel in place to stop her in case she thought to retaliate.

"What was that?" she whispered furiously as the first screw slid into place.

Her lips had been incredibly soft. He could still feel the contact. "For good luck," he said. Not that he really knew what the hell he was doing.

"I thought you didn't believe in luck."

She had him there.

"Just because I don't believe in it, doesn't mean we don't need it." Which made little sense. He hoped she wouldn't notice.

He made quick work of the screws, made sure nobody could tell anything had been tampered with. Then he emptied the two cardboard boxes he'd noticed earlier, distributed their contents on the shelves so the extra parts wouldn't be too obvious.

Separately, neither of the boxes would have been large enough to hide him, but next to each other, with one side taken out of each and the holes fitted together, he could squeeze in and settle into a semicomfortable position.

Which was probably still a lot more comfortable than Lauryn was, he thought, not without some guilt. "Are you okay?"

"Hunky dory," came the muffled reply.

Probably one of those Americanisms. "And that means?"

"Fine. I'm fine." She sounded decidedly snappish.

He thought it might be better not to annoy her any further so he remained silent. They spent an hour or so that way. In the end, she was the first to speak.

"How long do you think it'll be before they come?"

"They'll check on us soon. It's almost morning."

The sun did rise after a while. It shined right on his box, making him sweat.

Nobody came.

Finally, he heard the door open and shouting ensued immediately, spiced with a lot of Turkish swearing. Someone kicked the shelf. Istvan held his breath. If they kicked his boxes and they slid apart…

But the man seemed to have already spent his anger. The sound of boots running down the hallway came next.

He lifted the top of the box that held his upper body and stole a look. Then sat up and climbed out, careful not to rip the cardboard. If the men thought Lauryn and he had escaped the ship, they wouldn't begin a search. If they figured out the prisoners' ruse and realized that the two of them were still on the ship, they'd mount a manhunt for sure.

He put everything back together, then went straight for those screws in the metal wall panel. "Just give me a second."

But whole minutes ticked by before he had her out of there, then even more time passed as he rushed to screw the panel back into place. She was stretching her limbs in silence as he worked. They could hear voices by the time he was done, one of them the captain's.

He stuck his head out the door. The hallway was empty. The men were still around the corner.

"This way." He grabbed Lauryn's hand and dragged her in the opposite direction.

Chapter Five

Lauryn held her breath as she squatted behind a barrel at the end of the hallway that held the crew's quarters. She hoped her growling stomach wouldn't give her away if anyone was in hearing distance. She hadn't had any food or drink in two days.

But the hallway seemed deserted.

"I'll go and see what I can find," she told Istvan behind her.

"I'll go with you," he countered.

It had been his idea to come here and look for food after they found the kitchen well-attended and impossible to get into without drawing attention. He seemed to think that the crew must have had at least some snacks in their bunks.

Ready to see for herself, Lauryn darted forward in a low crouch. The door of the first cabin was open. Nobody in there. She was inside the next second and moved to the side, keeping in cover of anyone who might step into the hallway from one of the other cabins.

Istvan was right behind her, pausing for only a

moment to survey their situation before heading for the bunks. Four were crammed into the small cabin, the bedclothes he turned over smelling stale, carrying the odor of unwashed men.

Lauryn saw something under one of the bottom bunks and went for that, came up with a half-empty bottle of cola. She searched through a canvas bag next and found a fancy chocolate bar, probably a gift from one of the crew to his sweetheart back home. He could bring her another one next time, Lauryn thought and lifted that, too. Hopefully, the crew would blame each other. She moved on, but no matter how carefully she looked, she couldn't find anything else.

She shot a questioning look at Istvan when she was through searching. He held up a bag of dried figs as he nodded toward the door, apparently ready to leave.

She followed him.

He couldn't have cut it as a cat burglar, but he had some good moves for his size, had excellent instincts and amazing upper-body strength. Definitely not a palace weakling. Not counting his ever-present scorn for her, he was all right so far, although she would have preferred to work alone. She wasn't used to having someone by her side, especially someone who didn't trust her. It threw off her stride.

Under different conditions, she could and would ditch him at the first opportunity. He might have thought he was keeping her with him, but she stayed of her own will. Because during the time she'd spent walled up in the electric panel, she'd realized just how much she needed him.

Like it or not, her name was now connected to the biggest heist of the decade, if not the century. Rumors of her past *would* resurface. Worse, details of her father's past would be dragged to light once again. Her newly legitimate position in the art world had been delicate to begin with. A shadow of doubt would be enough to ruin everything.

And that wasn't all. The deal she had made with the FBI was good only as long as she stayed on the right side of the law. All investigation pertaining to her had been suspended. But Agent Rubliczky warned her that if he had the slightest suspicion that she stepped over the line, or was even thinking about stepping over the line, all bets were off and he would come after her with a vengeance.

If he did, she would be out in the open, defenseless. A lot of her old friends had cut her off, feeling betrayed when she'd left the shady side of the business. She couldn't count on that world hiding her again. And not all of her new acquaintances trusted her yet. If she was under scrutiny, they might not want to associate themselves with her and come to her aid.

She was alone. She'd been alone since her father's death.

It was a definite advantage, she told herself, as she always did when the loneliness got to her. Prince Istvan didn't trust her. He'd prefer to see her in jail than anywhere else. Almost enjoying his company was the most outrageous foolishness.

Her thinking would return to normal once their paths separated.

But she couldn't separate them yet.

She had to be firmly and visibly on the side of good. Personally on the recovery team, if possible. She needed to be at Istvan's side when he brought the stolen treasure back into the country. She needed to be in the pictures, needed a seat behind the table at the press conference. She had to talk him into letting her be there.

But now was not the time. Voices came from the hallway.

She swore under her breath. The crew couldn't have numbered over two dozen, a group that should have been insignificant on a ship this size, but it seemed they were constantly around.

She immediately stepped to an open window, larger than the porthole they'd had to deal with before, slipped outside and stood on the window frame. "Boost me up."

To his credit, Istvan did so without asking any questions. He pushed her high enough to reach a trailing chain and hoist herself up on deck. Then she watched as he came up behind her. As much as they could, they stayed on top, not knowing the outlay of the warren of hallways, cabins and storage areas below. She didn't like the idea of being trapped down there.

She followed Istvan, who was already climbing the nearest container. They both preferred higher ground.

He kept going, not stopping until he was on top of the container that was on top of the first. From here, they had a fair view of the ship and the sea, but were nearly invisible as long as they lay flat and kept away from the edges.

She set the bottle and the chocolate between them, he put the figs out there, too, then pulled a chicken drumstick wrapped in a greasy piece of paper from his pocket.

"Protein."

"I'm a vegetarian."

He looked at her as if she were out of her mind. "But this is an emergency."

"Principles are still principles. Even in an emergency. *Especially* in an emergency." Of course, he probably didn't expect someone with her background to have any principles. She absolutely hated the fact that she was beginning to care what he thought of her.

She drank some cola first, wishing for plain water instead of the sugary liquid, then ate a handful of figs.

"Eat it all." Istvan pushed the bag toward her. "I'll have the chicken. If you're sure."

"Very." She tended to cling to her convictions, a response to a life that she sometimes likened to a leaf blowing in the wind.

Her father, the work they did together, had defined her in her childhood then as a young adult. The change she'd had to make after his passing, the bargain with the FBI, had been more difficult than she'd expected. She had to change her life, her actions, her thoughts, everything about her. It was the ultimate paradigm shift.

She liked the person she was becoming. But from time to time, she still felt as if the ground wasn't one-hundred-percent solid under her feet. One of the reasons why she sought to define herself with lifestyle choices, she supposed.

Istvan wouldn't understand. He was a prince. His whole life had been defined for him the moment he'd been born. His foundations rested on a six-hundred-year-old royal dynasty. He certainly didn't seem to be troubled with any existential questions as far as she could tell.

The morning sun was peeking in and out from behind the scattered cloud cover, warm, but not unbearably so, its heat further mitigated by the sea breeze. He took off his jacket and offered it for her to lie on. She accepted. The corrugated steel was none too comfortable, and she knew they could be up here for hours.

When she ate the figs and he finished the chicken, they split the chocolate, then drank the last of the cola. Sharing the bottle felt strangely intimate. They were almost like old friends, sitting in companionable silence. But they weren't, she reminded herself.

"What about your mom?" he asked out of the blue, reclining on his side, watching her.

"What about her?" she shot back, caught completely off guard.

"I was thinking about how a person turns out like you. I already know about your father."

Her spine stiffened. *People like her...* So much for the brief mirage of the two of them as friends. "I turned out just fine." She was working on it, dammit, every single day.

"I never implied otherwise." An amused smile played above his lip. "Maybe I meant you were self-sufficient and quick on your feet." The sunlight glinted off his dark hair. His wide shoulders were outlined against the endless blue sea. His powerful body was relaxed, his full attention on her.

The whole scene had a surreal quality, almost as if they were on some romantic picnic, which couldn't have been further from the truth. They were stowaways on a ship filled with armed criminals.

"My mom died when I was young." She shared that much against her better judgment.

"How?"

She had no intention of telling him. She'd never spoken of that time to anyone, never intended to. But the way he was looking at her made it clear that he wasn't going to let the matter drop, so she decided to give him a sentence or two to satisfy his curiosity.

"She was killed. I don't remember much." She wrapped her arms around herself. "I don't like talking about it."

Of course, that didn't deter him in the least. He leaned forward. "Did it have anything to do with your father's occupation?"

For a second she considered saying car accident,

hoping that lie would cut off further questions. Then she decided against it and simply nodded.

"What happened?" He pushed as she'd feared he would.

She was already regretting telling him the truth in the first place. "My father had something someone else wanted. They took me and mom. He tried hard to get to us in time, but he was late."

She braced herself for more questions, determined not to speak another word of what had happened. But instead, he simply swept the garbage from between them and silently pulled her into his arms.

The gesture startled her as much as the brief brush of his lips had back in their prison cabin before they'd broken free. She was convinced that he couldn't stand her, yet this was the second time he wanted to comfort her and did so with an intimate gesture.

She pulled back and looked up into his face. "Why are you doing this?"

For a moment it looked as if he might pretend not to know what she was talking about, but then he said, "Damned if I know. I didn't exactly plan it."

"So what, you took me into your arms against your will?"

He grinned at her. "I'm a handsome prince, aren't I? I'm used to beautiful women throwing themselves at me. Whatever I do, don't take it seriously. You looked forlorn."

"I'm a strong, self-sufficient woman. I don't look forlorn. On principle." She pulled farther away. "Don't do me any favors."

His grin widened. "I didn't say it was strictly a favor. I said I didn't plan it."

He was impossible. Impossible to argue with, impossible to ignore, impossibly handsome. Beautiful, cultured, high-born women probably did throw themselves at him on a daily basis. And there was no reason on earth why the thought of that should annoy her.

She turned to the sea. She needed to quit engaging him at every turn. It wasn't as if he'd come on to her. He'd offered a moment of solace. End of story. He probably had someone waiting for him back at the palace.

"Don't you have a girlfriend?" European tabloids were always full of their princes' exploits.

From the corner of her eye she caught as his body stiffen. She turned back to him. The grin faded from his face. She'd hit a sore spot, obviously.

"Not really."

"She left you?" Curiosity got the better of her. "I can't blame her. Must be tiresome to kowtow to a prince 24/7. I know I couldn't do it."

He said nothing, a shadow passing over his face.

"Hurts the masculine pride, doesn't it?" She smirked. He'd been in full control from the moment they'd met, prejudiced against her and judging her without apology, so she enjoyed turning the tables on him. "Let me guess, she's an actress or a dancer or something."

His gaze darkened.

"No, no wait. The debutante daughter of a nobleman. Did you meet at court?"

"We met in a pit of mud," he said the words on a low voice but distinctly.

For a moment, she thought he was joking but the way his lips flattened hinted otherwise.

She kept the tone light. "How romantic. I didn't know you were a fan of mud wrestling."

If looks could kill…

"She was an archaeologist, the most honorable woman I know." He looked at her pointedly, then added, "A member of the Royal Valtrian Academy of Sciences."

She almost said, *How boring,* but that *was* caught her attention and kept her quiet.

"We met at an excavation. Her find." Pain came alive in his voice.

She couldn't have spoken now if she wanted to. The sudden vulnerability in his eyes made him seem more real, more ordinary, more approachable than she'd ever seen him before. His guard was down, for the first time since they'd met. There was a moment of connection where none had existed before.

"Amalia died last year. A tunnel collapsed on her," he finished.

"Were you there?" she asked at last, after a stretch of silence.

He shook his head somberly.

And she understood that it was part of his pain. That he hadn't been there when Amalia had needed him.

She felt the same at times about her mother. She'd

been there, but had done nothing. Granted she'd only been six, but she could have thought of *something*. Her father had been on his way. All she would have needed to do was find a way to delay.

"I was there with my mom. They hooked her up to an electric cable and made her scream into the phone for my father. I don't think they meant to kill her. She had a bad heart that just couldn't take it. I got loose and rushed to her. My fingertips got burned. And the top of my ears." She rubbed one absently. "That's why I don't like electricity," she whispered.

"I'm sorry." He seemed completely subdued all of a sudden, his gaze—filled with nothing but sadness—steadfast on her face.

She drew a deep breath, then scooted across the distance that separated them and slid back into his arms.

"Why are you doing this?" he murmured into her hair.

"Damned if I know. I didn't exactly plan it."

His comfortable warmth, the pillow of the nook of his arms and the gentle swaying of the ship made her sleepy. She had only rested in fits and starts in the past two days, always surrounded by danger. She wished they were off the ship and someplace safe so she could sleep.

The sun was low in the sky by the time she woke and found him watching her with an unreadable look on his face.

She blinked. "Did I miss anything?"

"There's land ahead." He pointed when she pulled away.

"Close enough to swim to?"

"Not yet, but we seem to be heading that way."

"Turkey?"

"Too soon."

Her mind was still fuzzy from sleep, surprised that she had nodded off, could sleep so soundly in the prince's arms. A strange rapport seemed to have developed between them when she hadn't been looking. She sure hadn't seen that coming.

They watched the land grow larger and larger on the horizon as time passed. Neither of them spoke, each trying to figure out if this changed anything.

Then Istvan broke the silence at last. "We're getting too close."

"Isn't that a good thing?"

His eyes narrowed to slits as he considered the landmass ahead. "The captain talked about Mersin, a Turkish port. Of course, that doesn't mean they didn't have any scheduled stops before that."

"You think the ship is going to port right now, over there? On some island?"

"On a large island. Looks more likely by the minute." He pushed up to a squat. "Let's go."

He moved to the edge of the container and lowered himself. Lauryn did the same. They were close to the side of the ship so they didn't have much open deck space to cross. They got in cover and waited.

When they were close enough to make out the row

of hotels sitting on a sandy beach, Lauryn climbed over the railing. He hesitated behind her. She knew why.

"You're not abandoning the royal treasure. You're going to get help so everything can be retrieved." She didn't jump until she saw him nod. Then she pushed away, fell by a couple of portholes and prayed that nobody was looking out and saw her.

She hit the water hard, went under but broke the surface again soon and immediately began swimming to get away from the current the ship's giant propellers churned up. Soon Istvan was there by her side and keeping pace. When they were at a safe distance, they stopped to tread water for a moment. At least the water was nice, it being the Mediterranean Sea at the end of summer. The sun was about to set. On the shore the lights were turning on one after the other.

"What do you think it is?" she asked, gesturing toward the island with her head, spitting out salt water.

He looked up at the cloudless sky where the first stars were coming out, and seemed to be orienting himself. "Cyprus."

Another wave splashed her face, but couldn't wash off her optimism. She loved Cyprus. Her uncle lived on Cyprus. She could ask him for help.

"So we made it, right?" She could have shouted with joy, but although probably nobody on the ship would have heard her over the noise of the giant propellers, she figured it was more prudent to celebrate quietly.

"Unless the sharks or the currents get us," he said,

seeming immune to her exuberance. "Or they spot us from the ship."

As if to underscore his words, shouting broke out on deck. Followed by bullets peppering the water all around them.

So they *had* been seen from one of the portholes, she thought, then drew a deep breath and swam for shore.

Chapter Six

In the end, it wasn't the bullets that got them, nor the currents, nor the fearsome sharks, but the lowly jellyfish. Istvan's skin burned as he climbed to shore. Now he knew how his brother Lazlo must have felt when he'd been trapped in a burning wreck at a car race. He could swear he felt the licking flames.

"How can something so small cause so much pain?" Lauryn sat on the sand next to him, pulling up her pant legs and blowing on the forming welts. Her wet shirt stuck to her like a second skin.

He glanced toward the hotel. "I'll go call for help. Stay here." He hesitated for a moment. "You *will* be here when I return?"

"I let you lock me in an electric closet." She rolled her eyes. "I would like some of that trust returned."

He waited a beat or two as he considered. Then he nodded.

"I'll go soak." She gave a soft moan as she rolled her pants higher, then stood to stride into the water up to her knees.

Salt water was supposed to be good for the stings. He'd be joining her as soon as he got back. "Be careful."

The patch of jellyfish were a few hundred meters offshore, but that didn't mean the waves couldn't wash some closer. They liked coming up to the surface at night.

He ran his fingers through his hair and squeezed as much water out of his clothes as he could without taking them off, then strode barefooted across the sand, going around rows of beach chairs and umbrellas. They'd both ditched their shoes in the water to make swimming easier. His fake mustache was gone, too, along with the rest of his disguise. They hadn't survived this last bit of swimming.

He walked right into the plush lobby and straight to the front desk, ignoring the curious stares from the guests. He kept his face from them, but couldn't do that with the front desk manager, whose eyes went wide with recognition. The man's hand flew up to adjust his tie. His back straightened. He drew a long breath and opened his mouth, no doubt for a ceremonial greeting.

"I need help," Istvan said under his breath before the man could have spoken. "And your discretion."

"Certainly, Your—" The front desk clerk caught himself and lowered his voice. "Certainly, sir." Even his graying mustache seemed to stand to attention.

"I've had a boating accident with a friend. I'll be with her on the beach. I need you to call the Valtrian Embassy and arrange for a pickup. Also if your security could keep the guests off the beach until we vacate it, I'd appreciate it."

The man bowed. Caught himself too late this time. Glanced around nervously. "Yes, sir."

"And I need your ID badge."

The white photo card was handed over without question. "Let me give you some privacy," the man said, then raised his voice as he addressed the guests milling in the lobby. Some were coming from dinner, considering a walk on the beach, others were meeting with friends to go out for a night of partying. "Ladies and gentlemen, we have an open bar at the Roman Lounge on the first floor at the back of the hotel. All drinks are on the house. We are happy to have you here. For the next hour, all drinks are free."

People began to move toward the back of the lobby, looking pleased and more than willing to be distracted.

Istvan turned on his heels and strode out, grabbing a couple of beach towels from a cart by the door, keeping his head down, avoiding looking at anyone who might have lingered.

He was relieved to see Lauryn still where he'd left her. He hadn't expected her to run—she was injured, without money or any form of ID in a strange country—but he hadn't been one-hundred-percent certain. She was good enough and troublesome enough to pull it off if she really put her mind to it.

He wasn't ready to let her go yet. He told himself it was because he still suspected her and he wanted to keep an eye on her until he figured out whether she'd had any part in the whole sordid heist business.

"How are your stings?" He draped a towel around her shoulders, the other one around his own.

"On fire."

"Help will be here in a few minutes. Lift your leg." He squatted before her and helped her balance with one foot on his knee while he ran the edge of the ID card along her skin to shave off any adherent nematocysts. "All right, let's do the other one."

To do the job right, he had to touch her. Her skin was hot where she'd been stung. He could feel the shift of muscles in her calf when she moved slightly. There were a few stings even on her thigh, the thin material of her pants having provided little protection. His jeans had done a better job, as well as his jacket. But his shirttail had worked loose while he swam, so he'd been stung around the abdomen. He was feeling a lot less of that pain now, however, as he did his damnedest to focus on her injuries and nothing else, certainly not the way moonlight reflected off her smooth skin.

"Let me help you," she offered when he was done.

"I got it." The thought of her nimble fingers on his lower abdomen was more than he could handle. He scraped the skin with painstaking care, making sure he got everything. "Now there won't be any more toxins released, at least."

"Neat trick with the card." She patted down her hair and squeezed water out of the ends. "Where are we in Cyprus?"

"I didn't ask." His main goal had been to arrange for help and get out before any of the guests recognized him. He glanced around and saw hotel security higher up the beach, on the large patio, turning guests back inside. They must have also escorted inside the handful of guests who'd been lingering at the edge of the beach when Istvan and Lauryn had reached shore. They were now completely alone on the stretch of sand.

"Thank God for the weather." Her hair arranged to her satisfaction, Lauryn moved on to dabbing the towel over her clothes to wick some of the water away from her body. "If we had a storm or if the water was cold, this could have been a lot worse."

He resisted the urge to offer help. "We'll have food, water and medicine soon. Hang in there." He scanned the road. How soon help would arrive was anyone's guess. The Valtrian Embassy was in Larnaca, the capital city. For all he knew, they were on the other end of the island. He could see several restaurants and hotels from where he stood, but as luck would have it, none had the town in the name.

He was craning his neck, trying to catch something he might recognize, so absorbed in the task that he almost didn't notice the black limo pull up ten minutes later, displaying a diplomatic license plate.

A uniformed chauffeur stepped out, along with a bodyguard. Istvan helped Lauryn out of the water and walked to meet the men halfway.

"Your Highness," they said at the same time.

"Thank you for coming. Where are we?"

"Porto Paphos." The chauffeur was better trained than to show curiosity either at the question or the disheveled state of his would-be passengers.

Porto Paphos. Should have figured. One of the major ports on the north side of the island, but not anywhere near Larnaca. "How did you get here so fast?"

"The ambassador is in town with his wife for the international cat show. And he's giving a welcome speech for contemporary Valtrian art at one of the galleries tomorrow morning."

Probably set up by Chancellor Egon. "Good timing," Istvan said, catching from the corner of his eye as Lauryn worked to roll down her pant legs.

"Should I call an ambulance?" the bodyguard asked, apparently having seen the welts already.

Istvan looked at Lauryn.

She shook her head.

"That won't be necessary. Have a doctor dispatched to the Duke of Oskut's estate along with a half-dozen guards from the embassy." He walked to the limo and then, seeing that Lauryn was uncomfortable with the men, told the guard to ride up front.

"How far are we going?" Lauryn asked once the divider was rolled up and the car was moving.

"Not far. Relax if you can." He reached for the minifridge. "Champagne or something stronger?"

"Plain water if you have it. And maybe some ice for the stings."

He poured mineral water into two tumblers and handed one to her, gave her another glass with nothing but ice, then picked up the phone and called the embassy, identified himself. "There's a Turkish ship by the name of *Suleiman's Glory* probably docking right now at Porto Paphos."

Once they'd jumped, he'd made a point of looking at the name painted on the ship's side. "I want it stopped and searched. All hands are to be held along with the cargo. Nothing is to be removed from that ship until I get to it in the morning." He hung up and took a drink. He needed a shower, food and at least a couple of hours of sleep. His brain was barely functioning. Lauryn, too, looked dead on her feet.

"Must be nice to have all that power." She leaned her head against the back of the seat, her lips tightly drawn. Didn't look like the ice she held to her leg was helping any.

He knew how she felt. "Now and then it comes in handy." He put down his glass. "They won't be going anywhere tonight. We can rest. Then tomorrow I'll come back to the harbor and take care of everything."

She sat up and looked at him. "*We*'ll come back."

"Your presence won't be necessary. I'll go alone." She needed rest and healing.

Her gold-green eyes narrowed. "You still suspect me?"

He considered what to say, what he believed at this point. She wasn't what he had expected. There were issues he needed to rethink.

"I can't believe you have to think about it," she accused before he could have said anything, hurt and fury in her voice. "People were shooting at us. I could have been killed!"

"I noticed." Yet, he still didn't like the idea of her around the coronation jewels. Especially because she seemed to want to be near them so badly, which did make her look suspicious.

She set her glasses in the holders. "You should be grateful I want to help you. It's no cakewalk, with all your—" She snapped her mouth shut and made a sound of frustration in her throat.

He turned to her fully, raising his eyebrows. "I'm *not* difficult to work with."

She stuck her chin out. "Like somebody would dare tell you, Your Highness?"

He turned away from her and dialed the phone again. She was obviously in an unreasonable mood. There was no point in talking to the woman.

"This better be urgent. The runner-up to Miss Valtria is waiting for me in the hot tub out back," his cousin said in way of a greeting.

He had cousins only from his father's side, twelve boys and three girls from the four uncles altogether, all younger than Istvan, mostly in their late twenties and early thirties. The girls were charming, but the boys were rakes, every last one of them. They were removed enough from the throne to escape the worst of public scrutiny and media attention, and they made sure to live the combination of their wealth, title and relative freedom to its full potential.

"Only the runner-up?" Istvan couldn't help a jab. "What happened to the winner?"

"We dukes can't always get everything that falls so easily to you princes." Alexander gave a good-natured chuckle. "Want to walk away from wherever you're digging right now and join us? You could bring the beauty queen. She'd probably come if you called her."

"I'm somewhat busy at the moment, but thank you for the invitation. I was hoping for another favor."

"Name it and it's yours if you let me off this phone in the next thirty seconds."

"The use of your estate in Cyprus."

Alexander, the Duke of Oskut, was in the movie business, one of the main benefactors of Valtrian cinema. He had filmed a documentary at a Cyprus country estate just outside Porto Paphos a few years back, fallen in love with it and purchased it on the spur of the moment.

"When?" he asked.

"Right now. I'm there."

"Say it's not so you can dig up my backyard. Tell me there's a beautiful woman involved. I want confirmation of female companionship."

"Confirmed."

Alex hooted like a common rodeo cowboy. "I'll ring the housekeeper to open the gates."

"*Now* will you tell me where we're going?" Lauryn asked when he hung up.

And, of course, she found fault with the answer, so the rest of the trip was spent in the same bickering mood that she tended to adopt every time he naysayed her.

Clearly she was the kind of woman who expected to get what she wanted or there'd be hell to pay. He was missing soft-spoken Amalia more by the minute.

He was still unsettled by Lauryn after having arrived at the estate and instructing the maid to show her to a room on the top floor. As a first order of business, he went to see about some more help. He made sure she had immediate medical assistance, food and drink, clothes, whatever she needed. The only restriction he placed on her was that she wasn't to leave the house without his permission.

Knowing her as much as he did by now, he was glad he wasn't there when that bit of news was delivered to her by the twenty-something knockout housekeeper. Leave it to Alexander to fill every position around him with aspiring actresses and models.

While the doctor applied some local herbal salve on Istvan's jellyfish stings—after having finished with Lauryn—the prince arranged for money and weapons and an early transport back to the harbor. Then he put down the brand-new, secured cell phone he'd received when the guards from the embassy had arrived and absentmindedly fingered the motion sickness bracelet Lauryn had tied around his wrist. One had come apart when they'd swam to shore and was lost at sea. He'd meant to remove the other one when he'd changed his clothing, but it had slipped his mind.

"I'll remain on the premises in case you experience any further discomfort, Your Highness." The doctor backed toward the door when he was finished.

"I'm fine. But do keep checking on Miss Steler."

He looked around the spacious suite once the door closed behind the man. Alone at last. He called Miklos and filled him in on everything that had happened.

"Arpad has some state occasion he can't miss, but Janos and I will be there by morning. Wait for us."

"I will." He wanted to bring in as few outside people as possible for the removal of the crown jewels from the ship. He didn't even want the royal guard to know what was in those crates, let alone the Porto Paphos Port Authority. Everything would be easier if he had his brothers there.

Istvan wished good-night to Miklos, then hung up, stretched out on the bed and stared at the Greek fresco on the ceiling. He thought the day over, everything that had happened since the hit on the treasury, trying to come to some conclusions about Lauryn, but didn't get far before he fell asleep.

His dreams were dark and hot, prominently featuring a very intriguing ex-thief. He was pursuing her. She had something of his. At times he would almost catch her, touch her, but in the end she always slipped through his fingers.

He woke to the certain knowledge that he wasn't alone in the dark room. He wished the weapons the guards had given him were closer at hand, but he'd left them clear across the room on an antique chest of drawers. He stayed still, looked through a slit in his eyes without moving his head.

Nothing.

Then, after a long minute, a shadow shifted toward the bed. A hand reached out, held something. A weapon?

He reached out and clasped the would-be assassin's wrist, yanked the arm up and the body forward until the attacker was sprawled on top of him, his free hand holding the other wrist immobile.

He was ready to roll in a wrestling move he remembered from his college days when he found his nose pressed against a soft neck with a familiar scent. The squirming body on top of his was too light for a man, and the curves, too, were unmistakable.

"Lauryn."

"That's not necessary." They spoke at the same time.

He flipped her anyway, not willing to let her weapon hand go, but put his body weight on the other one so he could reach for the light on the nightstand.

The bright light blinded him only for a second, then he could make out the folded piece of paper he'd mistaken for a knife in the dark. She was still wearing the clothes she'd swam to shore in. His gaze slid to hers, to eyes that were calling down the wrath of all the ancient gods of the island upon his head.

He should have let go right then. But her lithe body stretched below his awakened all sorts of sensations in a remarkably short time. And brought back his dreams where she'd always been a step ahead of him, always slipping out of his hands.

I caught you now.

He bent his head and kissed her.

He'd brushed his lips against hers before on impulse when he'd walled her in behind that metal panel in the ship's cabin. Afterward, he had no idea why he'd done it, was certain it would never happen again, grateful that she didn't make a fuss over his lapse of judgment. It proved that she could be sensible when she wanted to be, when she could overcome her argumentative nature.

But this kiss wasn't like the one before. This one he meant.

Few things could have surprised him more than her kissing him back. Need surged immediately and lust. If the wall behind their bed collapsed to reveal the archaeological find of the century, it couldn't have drawn his attention from her.

He let go of her wrist and brought his hand down to tuck her even closer. Her arms went around his neck.

Her mouth was hot and responsive, every touch of her tongue sending a new wave of desire through him. The strength of the heat between them caught him off guard. He wasn't the type of man to seduce every hapless female he came across, like his infamous cousins, of which the Duke of Oskut was the mildest.

Istvan had always been more focused on his work. Even his relationship with Amalia had been a slow and comfortable affair. But at the moment he could barely remember her or anyone or anything else. Lauryn filled his senses and his hands.

Before he knew it, her shirt was open and his face was buried between her perfect breasts. He drew a nipple in his mouth, the most natural thing in the world, his body—too long denied—growing hard as she arched her back beneath him.

"Tell me this is what you came for," he whispered with urgency when he came up for air. He didn't want to stop. He wanted her full cooperation and agreement.

But she gave a pained laugh. "I came to leave a goodbye note."

That sobered him enough to pull up and look into her face. "You were going to sneak out." Understanding dawned, disappointment coming close on its heels.

"Obviously, my sneaking skills are rusty." She tried to make light of it.

"I was very specific in my orders that you should not leave without my approval."

"That's exactly why." She shifted from him. "I want to work with you on getting back what was stolen, but I will not be your prisoner."

The air was cooling between them. He didn't want that. He pulled her back. "Let's not argue."

"You mean, I should just serve your needs like a good little subject of the crown without raising any objections? I have news for you. I'm not a subject of the crown." She was deliberately misunderstanding him. Her gaze was sharp now, all the softness gone form her mouth.

"That's not what I meant." Although, if she felt in an obedient mood, he wouldn't have objected. He drew a long, frustrated breath. "You kissed me back."

She shrugged. "I figured that might be the quickest way out of here."

That stung. "How far would you have been willing to go?"

"As far as necessary." She didn't even blink as she said that.

His body still ached for her. He had half a mind to put her to the test.

"Sorry." She slipped out of his grip, out of the bed. "The gig is up, I'm afraid. What's this?"

She was holding a page of his handmade copy of the Maltmore diary. Water had soaked the copy through, so he had laid each page out to dry. The secrets of the Brotherhood of the Crown were set out on every available surface.

"An old document I'm working on." He moved to get the page she picked up, but she danced out of reach. "I'll have that back," he warned her.

She studied the writing by the light of the lamp. "What language is this?"

"I'm not sure."

"Let's see." She raised an eyebrow. "Not a natural language. Looks more like code. Who wrote in codes? Secret societies. Let me think of a Valtrian secret society that could have a book that a strapping prince like yourself might be interested in enough to copy by hand and carry in his pocket." She tapped her forehead theatrically. "I'm guessing it's some secret book of the Brotherhood of the Crown. How am I doing so far?" She looked pleased as anything with herself.

On the one hand, he found her quick thinking incredibly sexy, watching her mind work a thing of beauty. On the other hand, he couldn't say her guessing his secret so effortlessly didn't annoy him.

"What is it about?" She tilted her head, a sparkle in her eyes.

"I don't know."

"You can't decipher it?" The question was put forth with such belittling intonation as if to say she would have broken the code on a single lazy afternoon with a hand tied behind her back if given half a chance.

"Of course, I can read it," he said and realized too late that he'd given himself away, which had been exactly her purpose. His mind was still too steeped in lust to follow her quick thinking.

"Okay, then let's try this again. What is it about?" she asked with a smirk.

He decided to tell her. In equal parts because he didn't want her to leave yet and because none of the diary made any sense anyway.

"It's a collection of poems and sayings. Like the *Song of Solomon* and the *Book of Proverbs* in the Bible."

She held the page out for him. "What does it say here?"

He let his gaze run across the marks. "The wealth of a nation is in the head of the ruler."

"Makes sense. The smarter the king is, the better off the country will be."

Yes, in some way, but the gems of wisdom were no help to him whatsoever. When he'd found the diary he'd been hoping that the clues would lead him to the treasure of the Brotherhood.

The original Brotherhood of the Crown was made up of eight princes who put Casanova to shame. The only thing that outshined their deeds in battle had been their deeds in the bedroom.

When the country went through a particularly difficult period of foreign invasion, their lovers supposedly gifted the young princes with massive amounts of their jewelry, as love tokens and as support for an uprising. Except, the princes were betrayed and the treasure had disappeared.

Lauryn held the paper to the light. "Which one is the word for *wealth?*" she asked.

He pointed it out.

"And *ruler?*"

He showed her that, too.

"Then this is the letter *E,*" she guessed correctly. Then asked a few more words and within minutes, literally, had the entire alphabet decoded, by which time he regretted ever giving her any information.

"So it says, *The wealth of the nation is on the head of the ruler.*"

"*In* and *on* were interchangeable in the old language."

She nodded. "This is interesting. Can I take these back to my room to read through them?" Her head was tilted, the light playing on her slim neck, reflecting off alabaster skin. Mesmerizing.

He very nearly fell for it, but in the end came to his senses.

"Absolutely not." He held out his hand for the page.

Her eyes narrowed. He expected one of her biting remarks, but in the end, she stuck her tongue out at him. "You're no fun to play with."

A bolt of desire shot through him. "Didn't hear you complain a couple of minutes ago."

The reference to the passionate kiss they'd shared made her cheeks tinge. *Interesting.* She hadn't seemed shy when she was kissing him back. Urgent need resurfaced quickly at the memory.

"Lauryn—"

She backed away from him, an intriguing creature of the night that begged further investigating. "Good night."

He hated to see her go, something he needed to consider later. He was going to have to straighten out his thinking and his unexpected attraction to her the first chance he had.

"Fine. Go back to your room and stay there," he told her. "How are your stings?" he asked belatedly, more than ready to give her thighs a close inspection.

Her impertinent response was, "None of your business."

As soon as she was gone, he called security to meet her in the hallway, escort her to her room and stand guard in front of her door until he sent for her in the morning. Then he stretched out in his bed, his arms folded under his head.

He could still taste her on his lips.

He had a couple of hours left until dawn, but sleep didn't come easily. It didn't come at all, in fact. So he got up at five, washed and called for a car and armed escort, then left for Porto Paphos without breakfast. He would wait for his brothers on the ship. It would take hours before he had the whole thing searched anyway. Beyond recovering the royal treasure, he also wanted to find some clues as to who was behind the heist. He wanted the man who'd ordered it.

He called the estate just as his car rolled into the harbor. Port Authority was already there, waiting for him. He could make out the Turkish ship by one of the loading docks.

On the phone, he talked to the guard in front of Lauryn's room, asking him to check on her. He could hear knocking. Knocking again.

"Miss Steler?"

He heard the key being turned in the lock and the door opening. Then silence for a moment.

"I'm sorry, Your Highness. She doesn't seem to be here. I can't find her," came the worried, embarrassed reply from the other end.

Pretty much what he had expected.

Chapter Seven

He hated to be right about her. Right in some ways, in any case. Wrong in others. She'd turned out to be an exceptional woman, possessing a lot more than the criminal brilliance he'd first attributed to her. For a second, as he walked across the shipyard, Istvan imagined what it would be like to work with her on a dig, deciphering ancient messages carved in stone. Her mind would be flying a mile a minute, that rapture of discovery on her face…

To work with her like that would be nothing short of exhilarating, he thought, and felt guilty. He'd used to do fieldwork with Amalia and he'd never once thought of her in those terms. He appreciated the warm companionship Amalia had provided, but his head had never been as full of her as it was with Lauryn. Even now, steps from reclaiming Valtria's royal treasures, she was the only thing he could think of, the way she'd come to his room in the middle of the night, the way her face lit up at the sight of the Maltmore diary.

The things that could have happened between them under different circumstances…

He could still feel her lithe body under his, taste her mouth, hear her laugh, hear her repeat some lines of the text. "The wealth of the nation is on the head of the ruler," she'd said.

His mind ground to a screeching halt, as did his feet. His guards nearly ran into him because they'd been following so closely, but he paid little attention to the puzzled looks they gave him.

On the head of the ruler.

He'd corrected her last night, but now as he heard her say the words in his head again, he got stuck on that small difference. *On,* as opposed to *in*. What if she'd been right the first time around? What if the Royal Brotherhood left clues to their treasure right on the royal crown?

What better place to hide that message? The crown was always well-protected. No one but the royal family had access.

Until now.

At the moment, the royal crown was on the ship ahead of him. He broke out running, everyone following behind.

"The crew?" he asked the Port Authority official who came to greet him. Suddenly he felt as if he didn't have a second to waste.

"Held in the canteen on the ship, under armed guard, Your Highness."

He strode across the plank onto the ship, then straight

to the containers in the general area where he believed the one they were looking for was located. "You and you—" He pointed at two of the guards behind him. "Climb this stack, get as high as you can. We're looking for a container that has one of its top corners peeled back." The small explosion Lauryn had created to get them out of there also marked the container, making his job easier now.

They couldn't just look for a door with two bullet holes in it. Most of the containers were crammed too closely together to squeeze in and check the doors on every one of them.

The men immediately dispersed and did as he'd ordered. He couldn't help but notice how much slower and clumsier they moved than Lauryn.

He had to wait at least half an hour before one of the men shouted down. "I got it." Then he led the group on the ground to the right location.

The container in front of his had been moved somehow. As if to allow someone entry.

He was going to wait for his brothers with the opening of the container, but he was unable to hold back now. He threw open the doors and strode in, adrenaline pumping through him. He would get everything back. The treasure was all safe. He willed it so.

But he could see within two steps that the contents had been disturbed. The tops of several crates had been tossed to the floor. He jumped up on the first, his skin burning where his clothes rubbed against his abdomen.

He barely noticed the pain from his lingering jellyfish welts.

Empty. The realization echoed through his brain.

He smacked his fist into the wood. "Search every crate," he ordered the Valtrian guards, while motioning Port Authority back. He worked alongside his men.

"Empty," one called out.

"Nothing here," said another.

"Bare-root roses packaged in sawdust," came the first response that was different.

Valtria's signature purple roses, a common export item, the official contents of the container that the ship's captain had declared toward customs as cover, Istvan guessed.

"Keep searching," he said, although he knew by then that all the effort would come to naught.

He turned away in disgust. He should have come earlier. He should have come right away last night. But he'd been tired, and he knew Lauryn had been tired. He'd wanted to see her safe and settled.

Then a familiar shape caught his eyes, Lauryn sauntering across the shipyard, dressed in all black, self-possessed and full of confidence. Catwoman had nothing on her. He came off the ship to meet her, ordering his men to search the entire ship and get the crew ready for interrogation.

He caught some of the Port Authority officers on shore looking her over and didn't approve one bit, frowned at the gawkers. Normally that was enough of a warning for anyone to heed a prince's displeasure, but currently had no effect whatsoever. Next to her, nobody even noticed him.

"Everything's gone," he told her matter-of-factly, determined not to show that part of him was glad she'd come back even as he wondered why she did, or if she had anything to do with the treasure's disappearance.

He didn't know when she'd left the estate. He didn't know when the crates had been emptied. Her involvement was more than possible. But if she'd come to Valtria for the crown jewels and now she had them, she'd be on her way, wouldn't she?

There was no figuring the woman out.

"I got here an hour ago. Everything was already gone by then."

He didn't even bother asking how she'd gotten on a ship under full guard.

"They probably handed off the stolen goods before the ship pulled into port," she told him.

And he had to admit that the ship having had a rendezvous off shore seemed the most likely explanation at the moment. They might have had the transfer set up for Cyprus, but changed that when their prisoners escaped, suspicious that someone might be onto them. Then, because the ship's manifest included Porto Paphos, they had to pull into port anyway.

Lauryn sneaking on the ship at dawn was one thing. But surely the guards would have noticed if someone tried to remove a dozen crates' worth of treasures. It wasn't as if that war chest could have been smuggled off the ship in someone's back pocket.

But even if Lauryn wasn't part of the group who'd made off with everything, she *had* left the estate during the night and she *had* come here. She *had* sneaked onto the ship and *had* checked the container. All that didn't exactly help when it came to trusting her.

"The pickup team probably had a local fishing boat that could come to shore anywhere and wouldn't be subject to inspection," she was saying.

She was right. She was sharp and quick. The smart thing was to let her help. Frustration coursed through him as he considered their new situation. "Which means the things they took could be anywhere on the island."

They were both careful not to mention what exactly they were looking for. The Port Authority men stood too close. Although a press release had been issued about the break-in at the Royal Treasury, it had been played down and no specific items had been mentioned. Istvan preferred to keep the extent of the heist under wraps while he investigated.

He watched Lauryn, her eyes narrowed but unfocused, her mind probably going at the speed of light. He didn't trust her motivations, but he couldn't deny that she could be an asset to him.

So when she said, "I'm going to stick with you until we see this through. But don't try to lock me up again," he simply nodded.

THEY WERE HOLED UP IN a villa in Porto Paphos, owned by one of Istvan's cousins, the duke of something or other. Her rooms had an unobstructed view of the sea out front and of an amazing pool out back. The grounds were shaded by date palms and inhabited by more cats than Lauryn had ever seen in one place. She liked cats. They were all over the island, but seemed to especially prefer the estate.

Valtrian guards, borrowed from the embassy, took up residence on the lower floors, securing the building. The top floor was reserved for her and the prince. They each had a suite of their own, plus another to be used as a war room. It was already furnished with giant maps of the island, two computers and stacks and stacks of papers. They had received a list of art and antiquities dealers on the island—legitimate and illegitimate—the name of every cop who could be bribed, the location of every nook that could be used as a hiding place for someone trying to lie low with stolen treasure.

When a prince asked questions, people responded.

Everything and everyone responded to the prince. *Including her body.*

Those kisses in his bedroom—where they could have led… It didn't bear thinking about. Except that, despite her best efforts, she hadn't been able to stop thinking about it, about him. She'd run because her own response to the man had scared her. Her casual attitude to his touch, to his seduction, had all been pretense once she recovered from melting completely.

She'd also run because no matter how much he was getting to her, she couldn't allow him to get the upper hand. No man was going to control her, not in any way.

He needed to understand that, the sooner the better. Putting her under house arrest, indeed.

But then she saw him at the harbor. And felt his frustration, shared it. She could have started investigating on her own. But the truth was, she needed his help. And if she was totally honest, she liked working with him. And so she had walked up to the prince. She could only hope she wasn't going to regret it.

She listened to Miklos on the phone, on speaker. He and Janos had arrived earlier that morning, helped to search the ship, then arranged for a quick extradition of the crew to Valtria and took them back, along with the ship's captain. Miklos would be handling their questioning there. The princes were adamant about keeping as much of the case under wraps as possible.

"The crew is not talking. Yet," Miklos added with optimism. "I'm working with them. Janos found a couple players in Valtria with good enough teams, we think, to pull off the heist. One boss is the guest of Great Northern Penitentiary at the moment. We'll go after the others. Shouldn't take too long between the five of us."

"The twins are back?" Istvan asked with surprise.

"Lazlo cut his honeymoon a few days short," Miklos said as if it was no big deal. "Rayne got sick or something in South Africa, so Benedek was bringing her back anyway. My lovely wife says the kids are about to have a little cousin, but I can't get anything out of Benedek."

"Leave the men to me," Istvan responded with sudden

force. "Enough of our people died at the treasury. I will handle the investigation."

"The Brotherhood—"

"Is out of business," he cut Miklos off with a quick glance at Lauryn.

Which set off her radar. The brotherhood? What about the Brotherhood of the Crown? Istvan had been reluctant to share anything every time the subject came up. Why? The Brotherhood of the Crown had ended with those princes' deaths two hundred years ago. Unless… She turned to look at the maps to make sure her face didn't give her interest and suspicions away.

"I can fly back and forth," Istvan added.

"You're on Cyprus. Focus on the connection there. Unless you want us all to come back over and work from Porto Paphos together."

"No." His response was sure and immediate. "I'll take care of what needs to be taken care of here."

Stubborn, she thought. Wanted to do everything by himself. She would have loved to have siblings. She would have loved that kind of support, to have someone care about her problems. Maybe he was the type who could never admit that he needed help.

Then something in Istvan's face made her think. His voice had been brusque, but worry sat in his eyes.

He wants to keep his brothers safe.

Her heart softened with understanding. He wanted them out of harm's way. And harm was a near certainty with the investigation. She'd heard the gunfight in the treasury. She'd seen the rifles the ship's crew had carried.

"Be careful. Duty and honor, our lives for—" Miklos was saying.

Istvan grabbed for the phone and pushed the off button before his brother could finish.

Too late, she smirked to herself, keeping her face averted. *Duty and honor, our lives for the people and the crown* had been the oath of the Brotherhood of the Crown. Well, well, well. Was it possible that the Brotherhood had been resurrected? She put an ambiguous expression on her face as she turned to look at the prince.

He paced the war room, his brows knit in a frown.

"Why are you still here?" He stopped and addressed her suddenly.

She figured the question was coming. She didn't have any illusions. Most likely, the only reason he'd agreed to let her help was because he wanted to keep an eye on her and it was easier if he kept her close.

She thought about what he would want to hear. *You tell people what they want to hear and they'll believe you all day long*—a lesson her father had taught her. But as she looked into his dark eyes, which watched her closely, she decided to go with the truth.

"I need to be clearly, publicly, visibly on the right side of this one. I worked hard on building a reputation in this business. If there's even a shadow of a doubt that I had anything to do with this heist, my career is over and I can never get it back again."

He remained silent as she weighed her words.

"The world of arts and artifacts is my life. It's the only thing I know. After my father's death, I swore I wouldn't live on the dark side of this business. I sweated blood by the time I could make an honest living from it. If I lose that, I have nothing."

He was still silent, but she stopped there with her explanations. Either he chose to believe her or he didn't.

"All right," he said after a while. "We'll work together. But a word to the wise, Lauryn. I live and breathe for my country and family. Without that, I have nothing. I will do anything to protect our future as well as our heritage." He paused, his gaze reaching to her soul. "If I say you stay in your room, you stay in your room. Don't cross me again."

From the moment she'd set eyes on him, her image of him was that of the gentleman prince. But now she could see that there was a dangerous edge to the man. A thrill ran through her unexpectedly. She quashed it.

For too long, she'd liked thrill and danger too much. That was the lifestyle she'd inherited from her father, a lifestyle that had brought both of them to misery and ruin. These days she made a point of staying on a slow and steady path.

Even if she was contemplating a short side trip at the moment.

"Do you have any idea how we should proceed?" Istvan asked.

"Maybe," she said with caution. "I know someone on the island who's not on your list. Someone who would actually help us instead of running when he saw us coming."

"Who is he? Where can we find him?"

She hesitated. Their partnership was still tenuous. The prince was unlikely to respond well to her conditions. But she cared too deeply about the man she was talking about to reveal his identity without proper reassurance.

"I want your word that his identity will not be revealed to the authorities, nor will he be prosecuted for any involvement with the current heist or in connection to any information you might find out about any of his past activities."

Istvan stiffened. "I will promise no such thing. Who is this man? An old partner of yours? An old lover?" His words were clipped, his gaze hard.

"Your word that he will not be pursued in any way."

"Give me a name." He stepped forward, that warrior in him coming out again.

She stiffened her spine. "Not without your word."

"I could make you tell me," he threatened.

And she didn't doubt him. Even if she judged him to be too much of a gentleman to harm a woman, he *was* on a mission for his country, and he had plenty of men downstairs to do his dirty business for him. "Not even under torture," she said, just to make herself clear.

"I can't promise anything if he had a part in the theft." Istvan shoved his hands into his pockets, the vein in his neck pulsing with effort to restrain himself.

"He didn't."

"How can you know that with certainty?"

"He knew I was going to Valtria. He knew what I was going to be doing there."

"And he would never put you in any danger? He wouldn't chance that you might be implicated? Are you sure you're that important to him?"

She didn't need to think about that. "I'm sure."

He took his time thinking over her offer. "If he's not involved in the heist in any way, I'll guarantee his anonymity," he said at last.

She watched him, considering whether she should trust him. A fine team they made, neither trusting the other. Yet they must achieve their purpose. Too much rode on retrieving the royal artifacts for both of them not to try their hardest.

"You have my word as a royal prince," he added, reading her hesitation. "Now, where is this mysterious man?"

"I'll take you to him."

HE HATED WEARING A disguise. Istvan smoothed his index finger over the new fake mustache he'd acquired. To go out in public without it carried too much of a risk. He couldn't chance being recognized now. And he couldn't take a royal escort with him either. Lauryn had been adamant that only the two of them could go wherever she was taking him.

"How much farther?"

The car rattled as he drove down a dirt road through

the most breathtaking countryside Cyprus had to offer. They were heading south from Porto Paphos through fields of sparse vegetation, nothing but a few olive trees here and there and the odd group of goats as far as the eye could see. Rocky hillsides broke up the landscape that possessed a stark beauty.

"Almost there." She hadn't yet given him a name or a destination, informing him of each turn of the road only as they came to it.

Then, when he was beginning to think they would never get to wherever they were going, he went up a small rise and could see bigger hills in the distance, with plenty of green covering the sides and large crosses dotting the ridge.

"There it is." She pointed.

He had to lean forward to figure out what she was talking about. Then, finally, he saw it. Another mile or so ahead, an ancient-looking building complex was carved into the rocky hillside. Little more than caves on the very top, the structure grew more and more elaborate as it reached the foot of the hill and spread out. The domed tops of the attached buildings and the double cross on top gave it away, as well as the men in brown robes that he could make out once they got closer.

"Don't tell me you're taking me to a monastery."

Her smile grew. She picked up the cell phone she'd received from Istvan. "We'll be there in a couple of minutes. Can you meet us at the gate?" she asked whoever picked up the other end. "They don't let women inside the walls," she explained to Istvan after she'd hung up.

So her ex-boyfriend or partner or whatever joined the priesthood. If any woman had the power to drive a man to extremes, she was it, he had to admit. Although the thoughts she'd been inspiring in him of late were less than holy.

The potholes in the road kept his thoughts from going too far in that direction. The area must have seen some nasty rains in the past couple of days. Car traffic was probably negligible up here, so nobody had hurried to fix the problem.

They reached the monastery at last and he could see a man come through the wooden gate just as he pulled the car up to park. The guy was in his late fifties, dark-haired and, from what his rolled-up sleeves revealed, in excellent shape. He wore drab slacks and a simple shirt instead of a monk's robe. Women probably thought him handsome.

Istvan grunted, not the least happy when Lauryn flew from the car and straight into the man's arms. He swung her around in the air with a deep belly laugh. He hugged her tightly, not seeming to care one whit that he was way too old for her and entirely inappropriate.

Istvan stepped out of the car and cleared his throat with some force. And they turned to him at last, the man keeping his arm comfortably around Lauryn's shoulder, keeping her close to him.

"This is the friend I told you about over the phone," Lauryn said, in no hurry to pull away from the guy.

"Arnie." The man stepped forward and offered his hand.

"Istvan." He felt a ridiculous need to make his handshake firmer than usual but resisted.

"Let's go for a walk." The man finally moved away from Lauryn, but she immediately went after him and laced her arm through his as they started up a path that went around the monastery walls, higher up the hill, toward three giant crosses that looked over the valley.

"Lauryn said you lost something of significant value and high profile." The man looked at Istvan's face closely, the calculating look in his eyes indicating that he saw straight through the disguise. "I have a fair idea what it may be, but we don't have to spell it out if it makes you uncomfortable."

He found the man's words patronizing, although they were said in an easy enough tone. Best thing to do was to be courteous, considering that he depended on the guy's goodwill at the moment. He simply nodded.

"There aren't that many people who could pull off the job," Lauryn put in.

"And even fewer who could commission something like this. I'm leaning more and more toward the idea that it was a commissioned job. Nobody in their right mind would risk so much without already having a buyer," Istvan added, picking his steps carefully on loose gravel. "If we could figure out who the buyer is— I don't suppose you heard anything."

"I'm out of circulation these days," the man said noncommittally.

Istvan waited. Lauryn wouldn't have brought him here if she didn't think they could gain some valuable information. "Anything you could think of would be helpful."

Arnie seemed to be considering, so Istvan left him to it. As the path narrowed, there was no room for him to walk side by side with him and Lauryn, so he fell behind. A mistake, since his gaze was immediately captured by her lithe figure and the sinuous way she moved up the incline. She could thoroughly capture and hold a man's attention without half trying. The woman was nothing but trouble.

She had certainly captured Arnie's at one point in the past as the man had hardly let her go since they'd gotten here. Even when they reached the top and he sat by the foot of the tallest cross, he pulled Lauryn down close to him. "You trust this one?" he asked her.

"Until further notice."

"Don't overwhelm me." Annoyance surged through Istvan. Who was the ex-thief here anyway? That *she* would question *his* character went beyond belief.

Arnie turned to him. And the glint in his hard gaze said that if Istvan proved to be trouble, he could and would be taken care of before he had a chance to hurt Lauryn. Great. How did *he* end up being the bad guy all of a sudden?

He said nothing, knowing there was nothing he could say or do to make the man hurry. Arnie had to make up his mind on his own. All Istvan could do was wait. And as he did just that, sitting by the other cross and leaning his back against its base, peace filled him little by little. The valley spread out before him was an oasis of serenity. The monastery had an aura that seemed to blanket everything.

His breathing evened, his muscles went slack. He didn't even mind the flat looks Arnie gave him now and then as the man examined him from under hooded lids.

"There is someone I used to know," Arnie said at long last. "Seems like he backed out of a major deal unexpectedly a couple of days ago. Caused a few ripples. He's not the sort of man who does that. Could be that something better came along."

"Or he got spooked by something, or fell out with someone on his crew. Any number of things could have happened," Lauryn responded. "But you don't think that's it."

"You always hear gossip." Arnie shrugged. "On this one, I hear nothing. That has to mean something. He's not a crew boss, by the way. He's a middleman. He passes things along."

"How can we find him?" Istvan asked.

"You can't."

"Could *you* find him?"

The man shook his head. "Not anymore. I don't run with that crowd these days."

"Do you know anyone who could?" Lauryn asked and then stood and started pacing.

"Nobody who would help you, not even if I vouch for you. It's a tight club, you know that. They don't like outsiders." He picked up a pebble and turned it between his fingers.

He was still thinking. That was something. At least he didn't say, "Sorry, can't help," and walked away.

Lauryn stopped. "You have an idea."

Arnie dropped the pebble. "It's not worth articulating."

"Please."

He made a face, held up his palms as if to say he was washing his hands of this. "Fernando."

Lauryn looked as if she knew exactly who the man was talking about, but Istvan had to ask, "Who is he?"

"Nobody knows exactly. Very few people have ever seen him. He's a purchasing agent for the biggest buyers." Excitement stole into Lauryn's voice. "Reclusive."

"I happen to know that he's laid up for a while in Brazil. He had another one of his plastic surgeries. Facial reconstruction, fingertips lasered off again, the whole works. Not many people know about this."

"How can he help us?" The guy definitely sounded like a step in the right direction.

"He wouldn't. He'd have you shot if you so much as asked questions about him." Lauryn grinned.

"Glad to see the prospect of that makes you so happy," he groused at her.

"It's not that. You could be him!" She laughed out loud now, obviously thrilled with whatever idea she'd come up with. "Only a handful of people know what he looks like. And he's constantly changing his appearance to stay ahead of the authorities."

"If there was a one-of-a-kind heist, even if done on commission for a buyer that wasn't his, Fernando is the kind to want to take a look at the loot anyway. He's not the type to shy away from a bidding war if he sees something he wants."

"I'll be Fernando." He caught on at last. If nobody knew what the guy looked like and nobody knew that he was out of commission for a while, Istvan could enter the world of underground stolen artifact trafficking impersonating the man, find what he wanted and hopefully get out before anyone figured out what he was doing.

"Brilliant." He flashed an answering smile to Lauryn, her optimism rubbing off on him. "Can you set up some meetings for me, as Fernando, with the top people in the business on the island? I have a list," he told Arnie, not wanting him to think that they expected him to do all the work.

The man picked up another pebble. "Maybe."

"You know you can. You know everyone." Lauryn moved closer to the man, true affection reflecting in her clear eyes. "Everyone trusts you."

"Because I don't betray them," Arnie said in a sour tone. "If I do this. I'm going to have to leave here. I can never come back."

The smile slid off Lauryn's face. And Istvan understood that this was some sort of safe haven for the man, an escape he'd likely planned for years, a retirement he'd set up for when he would withdraw from the business.

"I know I'm asking you to risk your life," he told the man. "If you help, know that you have a place in Valtria and my protection." That was as close as he wanted to come to admitting who he was.

Arnie didn't look impressed. He looked ready to walk, in fact. But then Lauryn squatted in front of him, took his hands in hers and said, "Please."

His shoulders slumped as degree by degree the man gave up resisting. "I'll see what I can do."

Lauryn threw her arms around him in a warm embrace that twisted Istvan's guts for a second. He should have felt grateful and relieved. But he couldn't get past the annoyance at their frequent and ample display of affection. Could these two keep their hands off each other for a minute?

"You'll be Fernando." Lauryn stood at last and turned to Istvan, practically jumping with excitement. "I'll go with you. On the rare occasion when Fernando does business personally, he always travels with one of his mistresses."

"No," Istvan and Arnie said at the same time.

"You should stay at the village." Arnie nodded toward the two dozen small houses in the valley, white-washed walls and blue roofs, a postcard image of Mediterranean tranquility. "I can keep an eye on you here."

"On second thought—" Istvan turned to her. "I think it would be all right if you came with me. You could be of help. Definitely."

Chapter Eight

"I love banana fields."

They were on their way back to Porto Paphos, the car rattling over a road that looked like the moon's surface. Lauryn gazed out at the countryside, pointing out a shepherd or an old chapel now and then to keep the conversation going. Despite their first real breakthrough, the prince seemed to be in a mixed mood, saying little beyond cursing the deepest potholes.

"I don't think your Arnie likes me," he said absently, seeming unimpressed by the beauty of the banana fields.

They were in an SUV, a comfortable car with more than enough space, yet his physique and presence seemed to fill it to the brim. He was masculine without putting on any macho displays, handsome without seeming to be aware of it and intelligent without the need to show off his smarts at every second to impress her. He was also grumpy at the moment. And he could be bossy. Definitely a strong tendency there. Still, nobody could say he wasn't interesting.

"If he didn't like you, he wouldn't have helped," she told him.

"Maybe you didn't notice the way he was looking at me."

Maybe. But she'd certainly noticed the way the prince looked at Arnie. Of course, considering the business Arnie had been in prior to his retirement, perhaps Istvan's dark looks were understandable. "He doesn't like it that you're taking me into danger. I'm his only niece. He's allowed to worry."

The car slowed as Istvan turned toward her. "He's your uncle?" The look on his face was comical. It was the first time that she'd seen him truly confused.

"What did you think?"

He turned back to the road and accelerated. "Old partner or whatever. There isn't much resemblance."

Her uncle and her father had been dead ringers for each other. She took after her mother.

"Decent of him to help us. We'd be up the creek without a paddle if he didn't." He was beginning to sound appreciative. "Maybe he was right. You could stay. It'd be safer." He pulled onto the highway, the road much smoother here, and the car picked up more speed. "You could pack your things at the estate and I'll have a car bring you up to the village tonight. Looked like a nice place."

She actually did have things to pack. Before they'd headed out this morning, he had called a store and told them her dress size. They delivered an armload of clothes including accessories within the hour. Apparently, they were used to such calls coming from the Duke of Oskut's estate.

Right now, however, there was too much going on for her to enjoy the thought of her new wardrobe. Like the prince's sudden newfound mistrust. She'd really hoped they were past this. "An hour ago, you thought it was a great idea for me to come with you. Now you don't trust me enough to take me along? You do know you're driving me crazy?"

"You've been through enough danger in the past two days. It wouldn't hurt to at least try to stay safe and get some rest while you're at it."

"I'm going."

He considered her for a second before returning his attention to the road. "You really shouldn't."

"Oh, well. We're past that now."

He looked back at her, his eyes narrowing.

"Don't even think about it." She bristled, her mood mirroring his.

"What?"

"Putting me under house arrest again."

He said nothing, obviously remembering how easily she'd sneaked out the first time. He didn't look pleased at the memory.

Tough cookies.

Long minutes passed in silence as he drove. There were plenty of tourists out on the main highway, not all of them used to driving on the left side of the road, judging by the guy who pulled out from a side street straight into oncoming traffic. Horns blared.

The prince cleared the obstacle with ease. Then he drew a breath of resignation. "So you'll be my mistress."

There was something in his voice as he said those words that didn't sit well with her. "We'll be pretending," she reminded him.

BY THAT NIGHT, THEY HAD an appointment with Geoffrey Bellingham, the man Arnie had told them about. Bellingham agreed to a breakfast meeting the following morning. Turned out the guy was a British expatriate who had his operations set up on the north side of the island.

Istvan and Lauryn moved into a five-star hotel as if only having arrived, and shared a suite. Two of the most beefed-up royal guards dressed in black suits and black shirts took the next room as bodyguards. Fernando traveled with staff, so that fit right into their cover. Istvan would have preferred his cousin's familiar estate which provided more room and privacy, but they would be checked out thoroughly by Bellingham's men. He needed to act like the man he was impersonating, and five-star resorts seemed to be Fernando's usual home away from home when he traveled.

His guards were in their own room at the moment, Istvan picking over the remains of dinner that had been delivered to the suite, waiting for Lauryn to come out of the marble bathroom that was on par with those at the Valtrian Royal Palace.

His cell phone rang. The call came from his cousin's

estate, from the men he'd left behind. While he was going after Bellingham, he put an investigative team on his other suspects on the island. He didn't dare contact local law enforcement for help. He didn't know who could be bribed, which officer the bad guys might have in their pockets—according to Arnie, most of them.

"We have initial results, sir."

"Proceed."

"Costas is in jail. Has been for four months."

That left four more to worry about if Bellingham didn't pan out. "How about the rest?"

"Petrov is visiting family in Russia. Nobody's seen him for a month. He's said to be attending his sister's wedding."

As good an alibi as any. "And the other three?"

"Halil is keeping a low profile. Has some trouble with his crew. His second in command made moves to overtake the business."

So maybe Halil had other problems now and wouldn't attempt a major job.

"How about Berk and Canda?" According to the preliminary reports, both were of Turkish origin and known for their part in the black market artifact trade on the island. That gave them a possible link to the ship.

"Can't find either of them."

"Look harder," he said as the bathroom door opened.

Lauryn wore sensible cotton pajamas, well-fitting but not revealing. Part of him wished she'd picked something sexier from the pile the store had sent over. He hung up the phone. At least she hadn't come out wrapped in a robe to her chin, although in hindsight, he should have known she wouldn't. A shy woman couldn't have worn those Catwoman outfits that seemed to be her favorite.

She was comfortable enough in her own skin to dress any way she pleased. He liked that about her.

"So you'll be pretending to be my mistress," he spoke aloud the thought that waltzed circles in his mind while he'd been waiting for her. "Can you act? If either of us takes as much as one misstep, our lives are over."

One perfect eyebrow slid up. "If you're going to try to use that cheesy excuse to talk me into *practicing,* I'll be seriously disappointed."

Protesting would have only served to make him look guilty. And he wasn't about to admit that, yes, there was a sense of expectation in the back of his mind, his body buzzing now that she was there in the room with him, the enormous bed within reach.

"We have to look and act the part," he said simply.

She watched him for a long second, assessed him. Then her lips curved into a seductive smile. When she moved, there was a world of promise in her undulating curves. Slowly, tantalizingly she walked up to him. She straddled his lap, ran her fingers through his hair, never taking her eyes off him. She took his face between her hands, dipped her lips to his and kissed him.

There was nothing shy, tentative or simpering about her. She knew what she wanted and she took it as if he belonged to her. He found the kiss the most erotic of his life, and for the first time considered that maybe his brothers were right and he should spend more time in the company of women than in the company of centuries-old bones.

They'd accused him on more than one occasion of passing through the sea of ladies always present at court like a sleepwalker, barely noticing any of them. He was well awake now, conscious and alert. His body responded fully, passionately, his hardness pressing up against her soft core. His hands went to her waist to hold her in place.

Practicing seemed like a brilliant idea all of a sudden. He was looking forward to lots and lots of practice. It was the only path to perfection after all, as his father had been fond of saying.

But she was pulling away already, looking unaffected save for the smirk on her freshly kissed lips. "I think we can both make it look authentic."

He took a moment to collect himself. If she could walk away from this, then so could he. "How are your stings?" he asked when his breathing was semi-steady.

His had stopped burning, but they still itched.

"If that's a pitiful attempt to get me out of my pajamas so you can check, it's not going to work."

He couldn't help a grin. "What can I do? You're too smart for me."

"And don't you forget it." She sauntered to the obscenely large bed and lay right in the middle, then tossed a pillow at him.

"What's that for?" He knew he was slow on the uptake, but he couldn't help it. His mind was still addled; all he could think of was joining her on that bed and finishing what they started. That was the last thing he should have wanted under the circumstances, considering who she was and why they were here.

"For you on the couch. I wouldn't want you to be uncomfortable. You need to be fully rested for tomorrow." She gave him a cheeky grin.

"YOU SHOULD HAVE STAYED at the hotel," Istvan told her.

They were on their way to see Geoffrey Bellingham, sitting in the back of a limo while his guards rode up front. Bellingham took breakfast appallingly early. Istvan stifled a yawn. He'd barely slept the night before. Lauryn was not easy to ignore when sharing the same suite.

"We've covered this. We'll do the social thing with this guy, but I'm sure I won't be invited to the negotiating table. While you're with him, I'll wander around and see what I can see."

"The hotel would be safer." While he'd been lying on the couch and staring at the ceiling, he'd had plenty of time to think about, among other things, the danger he was taking her into.

"You were fine with me coming when Arnie offered to keep me safe in the village."

He didn't respond to that.

She watched him closely. And her eyes went wide

after a few seconds. "You thought he was an ex-boyfriend, didn't you?"

Should have known that she would work that out sooner or later. She had an amused look on her face. She clearly enjoyed having fun at his expense. Needling him was quickly becoming a hobby of hers. He couldn't say he minded it. He rather enjoyed their usual irreverent banter.

He wouldn't, however, give her the satisfaction of admitting anything. "Of course not."

"You didn't want to leave me with him." She grinned.

"Don't be preposterous. I'm not jealous of your uncle."

"You didn't know he was my uncle." She watched him with a speculative glint in her eyes.

"I talked to Miklos again earlier while I waited for you at the car."

"All right." She shot him a knowing look. "I'll be a good girl and play along. What did he have to say?"

"The ship's captain killed himself before he could be interrogated."

The blood left her face. "Why wasn't he secured?"

"He was. Looks like he ran full force into the brick wall of his cell and cracked his own skull. It's the damnedest thing."

"Whoever he worked for, he had to be pretty frightened of the guy." She rubbed her temple. "The rest of the crew?"

"Scared stiff and not talking." A moment of silence

passed between them before he continued. "Miklos had information on our Fernando, as well." Information Arnie must have known, although Istvan couldn't blame the man for not revealing it. "Apparently, when he gets tired of a mistress, he's known to leave her behind at a negotiation as a gift to seal the deal."

She blinked. "You're making that up."

He looked her straight in the eye. "Not hardly."

"If you dare—" She drew a deep breath.

He could see as she gathered steam. But even as she opened her mouth to give him some of her undiluted opinion, the car came to a halt. "We're at the lion's den," he told her. "Time to go in and do the bearding."

Truth was, he couldn't picture himself leaving her behind anywhere, not in the near future. He enjoyed her company too much. But at one point, he *would* have to give her up, he reminded himself. He was a prince. She was an ex-thief.

One of his bodyguards opened the door. Istvan stepped out first, then held a hand out to help Lauryn. She put on her mistress persona without a pause, linked her arm through his, pressing herself against his side as they walked, the thunder on her face seamlessly converting into a coy smile.

And he immediately realized what a huge distraction she would be. Yes, he could use her sneaking-around skills, but he couldn't shake the feeling that bringing her along might turn out to be a dangerous mistake.

Chapter Nine

Bellingham's home looked like a perfect English manor house both on the outside and inside, including a mahogany library with a fireplace, which, Lauryn suspected, didn't see much use given the climate.

The maid poured their tea, then left without raising an eye to anyone present or uttering a single word. Their host didn't acknowledge her either, certainly didn't thank her. He'd acted the upper-crust English nobleman from the moment they'd arrived. Probably wanted to make a good impression on the elusive Fernando. She knew Prince Istvan could outclass him in manners and in every other way, but he held back and acted the wealthy South American black market genius with aplomb.

"It's nice coming here this time of the year. Hot, but not any hotter than at home," he was saying as he lifted his cup to his mouth.

Bellingham's movements were more measured as he took in Fernando and his mistress, his gaze lingering on the soft silk dress Lauryn had selected for their breakfast, nearly sheer and snuggled close to the skin to accentuate every curve. She'd long ago learned the power of a good distraction.

She sat close enough to Istvan so their thighs touched, and made a show of paying attention only to him. But while she glanced up at him coyly from under hooded eyelashes and flashed him one bedroom smile after the other, she cataloged the contents of the room with a focus that wasn't easily won.

Plenty of bookshelves, but save an ornamental antique desk—Louis the Fourteenth, original—she found few signs that the place was Bellingham's working office. No computer in sight, for one. And she didn't see any filing cabinets either.

"I've heard a lot about you," Istvan was saying, faking a South American accent as best he could. "I regret that we haven't met until now. I'm not one for the social scene."

"So I've heard." Bellingham chortled. "You have the reputation of a hermit." His eyes narrowed. "All the more intriguing that you would stop by on a visit."

Istvan put his left hand on Lauryn's knee, then lifted it away slightly, hovering an inch or two above before allowing a finger to make contact again and trailing it up her thigh. Her skin heated from his touch, caressed by both his fingertip and the silk. Need snatched her breath away for a second before she could steel herself. He gave her a meaningful smile as he drew his hand back, the kind that would pass between lovers, full of promises.

She rose, acting on his silent message. "I'll leave

you gentlemen to your business. I saw a garden in the back as we came in. Would you mind if I explored it?" she asked their host, toning down the open heat, but remaining sufficiently flirtatious.

"Make yourself at home." The man's gaze dipped to her cleavage. "You may explore anything you like for as long as you please.

"You're a lucky man." She heard him say as she closed the thick wooden door behind herself. She didn't catch Istvan's reply if there'd been any.

Istvan's two guards stood at one end of the hallway, Bellingham's two men at the other. They looked her over, but didn't interfere as she walked toward the French doors that led to the courtyard in the back. She could still feel the prince's touch and cursed her attraction to the man.

Given her past, men in her life had been few and far between. She could never fully trust any, could never take anyone home to meet Daddy. She could never be sure if someone pursued her because he was an up-and-coming rival and wanted her secrets or an undercover cop trying to gain her confidence to collect evidence against her.

Both had happened.

She learned and never allowed more than a couple of dates, always stopped short of a true relationship where she would have had to share things that were personal.

Her dating habits left her lonely and frustrated, but she told herself she didn't have time for a man in her life anyway. First because her father had made sure her schedule was always full, and now because it took a hundred and ten percent of her energy to establish some kind of normal, legal career.

The last thing she needed was this unrequited attraction to the prince who'd just as soon see her tossed in jail than accept her help. She was walking the tightrope with him. She had to remember that. And the fact that his affection for her, so openly displayed in front of Bellingham, was all pretense.

Okay, not *all* pretense. He'd seemed plenty interested in her on multiple occasions when they'd been behind closed doors and not performing for anyone's benefit. His kisses... *Anyway.* Whatever attraction there was was none too deep. Most likely, he sought only to satisfy his baser urges.

She drew her lungs full of fresh air, pushing the prince and the way he made her feel out of her mind. She was famous for her razor-sharp focus. She called on that as she continued walking.

The garden walls threw enough shade in the morning to make the walk pleasant, so she followed the brick path that wound its way around palm trees and giant prickly pears, enormous bushes of flowering rosemary that had the bees buzzing. A marble fountain sprayed water in the center, the mist further cooling the air. She ignored the fountain and walked the perimeter instead, pretending to admire the plants while surreptitiously looking in every window.

She found the kitchen, a formal reception room,

storage rooms, bathrooms and, finally, the office. Little red dots indicated the cameras in the corner. The security system was on. No surprise there.

She didn't linger much longer, not knowing how long the prince's negotiations with Bellingham would take. She headed inside, right past the man's guards.

"I need to use the little girls' room." She smiled coyly, bending forward enough to let the neck of her dress gape. She drew the back of her index finger down her skin, toward the spot that grabbed the guards' attention. "It's getting hot out there. Would be nice to splash some water on my face."

One of the men gestured toward the end of the hallway, and she headed that way with a thankful smile. They didn't follow. They wouldn't move from the library door while their boss was in there with a stranger, she suspected. And they didn't have to follow her in any case. The hallway had its share of security cameras, giving a view of her activities to whoever was watching the monitors.

She walked into the bathroom as if she had no cares in the world, scanned it and was relieved that at least here privacy had been preserved. No cameras anywhere.

Which did seem kind of lax, considering that she'd seen them everywhere else in the house so far. She took a fresh towel and wet it, dabbed the cool cloth down her neck as she looked around, slower this time, pretending to enjoy freshening up a little.

She caught a suspicious dark spot in the painting that hung overlapping the mirrored back wall. She let her gaze glide right by as if she hadn't noticed. Then she wadded up the towel and placed it on the glass shelf below the picture, making sure it blocked the hidden camera's lens. She did one more sweep of the place, but couldn't find anything else.

The window was connected to a motion detector, but that was switched off, probably so the bathroom could be aired out if needed. She imagined they only turned the sensors on at night when they secured the premises. She looked out at the garden. The office she'd seen was right next door. If the window sensors were turned off during the day, she could climb out here and climb in there.

The garden stood empty, just as when she'd left it. The main danger came from being spotted through one of the other windows if anyone was watching. She made sure she checked every window she could see, but detected no shadows or movement behind any of them. The library was on the opposite side of the garden with Bellingham and Istvan, but Bellingham had been sitting with his back to the window when she'd left them.

In any case, this was her only chance, and the risks, such as they were, would have to be taken.

She opened the window, careful not to make a sound, and leaned out. She still couldn't see signs of anyone else. She vaulted out in one quick move, making sure she didn't tear her dress. Nobody shouted at her to ask what she was doing. She pulled the bathroom window closed.

A quick swipe at her bra produced a pick that helped

to open the office window. Then she was inside and closed this window behind her, too. Nothing should look amiss from the outside. The camera sensed motion and its red light blinked. She knew this model. Took about three blinks before recording started.

She dived forward and grabbed a handy little gadget from the other cup of her bra, held it up to the keypad and pushed a button. It temporarily overrode the circuits, tricking the sensors into believing that all was well in there. The red light on the camera stopped blinking.

She went to work immediately. Her gadget would work for only five minutes before the slight magnetic charge wore off. To use it a second time would risk permanently damaging the circuitry, which would be discovered once they left. She preferred not to blow their cover. They might need it again.

She went straight to the laptop on the desk, working in order of priority. She pulled a sticker from her bra with one hand as she turned the laptop over with the other. She pulled off the original barcode, stashed it and replaced it with her own. How many people ever checked the old factory stickers on the backs of their computers? Her sticker concealed a transmitter chip, a cloner. With the corresponding receptor, they'd be able to see everything Bellingham did on this laptop, now and forever.

Done with that, she tried the desk drawers. Locked. No match for her picking skills, however. She did a quick look-through, hoping to find a small artifact from the treasury, something Bellingham was possibly prepping for shipment or still evaluating. But there was nothing there.

The filing cabinets came next, yielding nothing relevant. Then she looked for the safe and found it cemented to the floor. There'd been a time when those floor vaults were very fashionable. She knew what to do, although this type wasn't one of her strengths. She ended up wasting precious seconds and found nothing but cash in several currencies and a half-dozen passports with Bellingham's picture but different names. She made sure to memorize them.

She was almost done when she heard footsteps outside the door. She glanced around with desperation for a hiding place as her heart rate tripled.

"WOULD IT BE FOR YOUR private collection or for a client?" Bellingham asked in response to Istvan's hints that he was looking for something extraordinary, one-of-a-kind pieces that might be floating out there.

"A client." He tried to look calm while his blood pressure inched up. He'd seen Lauryn climb in a window, but she hadn't come out. "An old client had come into some money recently and he heard rumors of certain items that don't usually come onto the market."

"Items like that are retrieved for specific clients, on order. More often than not," Bellingham added, his attitude remaining nonchalant.

"But if another buyer surfaced? I've yet to see a bidding war that was bad for us agents." He gave a short, conspiratorial laugh.

Bellingham nodded, his lips tugging up at the corners. "What sort of artifacts would your client be interested in exactly?"

Istvan dragged out the moment as if reluctant to reveal even that much. "He fancies himself the king of the underworld. Don't they all?" He chuckled again.

Bellingham's eyes narrowed. "And what brought you to *my* door?"

"Your reputation for one. If there's anything out there, I thought you might have heard of it. But I'll be making the rounds elsewhere, as well. I've heard a rumor that something somewhere might have disappeared. Somebody has to know where it went."

"Let me see what I can find out." Bellingham stood. "I hear you're a fan of Cubist art. I have a collection upstairs if you care to view it."

Istvan's heart about stopped. Lauryn was finally climbing back out the window. And Bellingham could turn any second.

"A wonderful library you have," Istvan said quickly, pointing at the shelves opposite from the window to draw the man's attention elsewhere. "I have lately grown to appreciate rare volumes myself. Another vehicle for investment."

"Feel free to look around," Bellingham said with pride in his voice.

Agents also being collectors wasn't that unusual. They started with lots they couldn't sell, then invested in better pieces over the years, as well. Having inventory on hand didn't hurt when they had clients with predictable tastes. Orders could be filled that much quicker.

"Look all you want." He indicated the room with an outstretched hand, turning in a circle, just missing Lauryn as she closed the second window behind her.

"I ALMOST GOT CAUGHT at the end. Somebody was coming into the office, but I skipped out the window while they fiddled with the lock. I've never been so grateful for a stuck key. What do we have so far?" Lauryn asked from behind Istvan.

They were back in their hotel suite, watching the screen change on the laptop in front of them. They had remote access to Bellingham's files.

"Enough to put him away for life, but nothing that would connect him to Valtria's royal treasures. He put out feelers after we left. His e-mails are vague. He's fishing around. If he found the stolen artifacts first, he could get a commission and I've given him the impression that my buyer is a grateful man."

"So even if he's not our guy, he's at least working for us."

He smiled, a glint of excitement in his dark eyes.

She felt the same. The hunt was on. To pursue her goals to the end was a challenge that gave her energy. She enjoyed every moment of the job. And judging from the look on Prince Istvan's face, maybe they weren't so different after all.

He'd already set up another meeting for tonight, with one of the two men who looked like the best bets out of the five black market bosses on the island. Berk was originally from Mersin, the Turkish port where the ship they'd taken to the island had been headed. It could be a connection or nothing more than coincidence. A link they planned to investigate, in any case.

"Dinner before we go?" Istvan asked her.

"Here?"

They'd been taking their meals in his suite, not wanting to take the risk that someone would recognize him despite the disguise. Their seclusion also fit their cover. Fernando was a man known to keep to himself.

He nodded, holding her gaze, and she had a feeling that this invitation was different than the ones before. She said yes anyway.

He made the call to the concierge and this time didn't invite his guards to dine with them, although his suite had a large enough dining room for a private party. The table for twelve was made of mahogany, a crystal chandelier overhead, the place also suitable to serve as a meeting room in a pinch.

He took off his jacket and unbuttoned the top button of his dark blue, tailored shirt, rolled the sleeves up to under his elbows, then took the chair at the head of the table and leaned back casually.

"I hope you don't mind if I don't sit on the other end." She picked a seat halfway down the table from him.

"Not at all. In fact, I'd prefer you closer."

His voice tickled something behind her breastbone. But his face was unreadable, and she couldn't be sure if there was any hidden meaning behind his words, or if he was simply stating that he didn't expect her to stand on ceremony.

She didn't have time to work out what all of it meant, the private dinner and his strange mood. The food arrived with super speed. Apparently, being rich enough to take the most expensive suite came with its privileges.

The waiter pushed a cart in, left it just inside the door without looking up once, as before, and was gone before they could have thought about a tip.

Istvan stood to serve them—one of his guards had done the job before. She jumped to head him off and take over the task. Her nerves seemed on edge suddenly, unreasonably. She wanted to move, do something that kept her busy.

She set the table and realized it'd be smarter to sit closer to him so they could both reach the platters they received. He made no comment, simply watched her, which made her nervous and then angry. She didn't get nervous under any man's gaze. She'd faced down Agent Rubliczky, for heaven's sake. Not to mention a number of rivals over the years, and even an amorous mob boss who hadn't taken kindly to being told no when he asked for a date.

She lifted the first silver lid. "Tava," she said as she recognized the dish, a stew of meats with onions and herbs, her uncle's favorite. The next dish was stuffed grape leaves.

"Vegetarian dolmades." He shook his head as if not knowing what to make of them. "Stuffed with seasoned tofu."

He hadn't asked her what she wanted, and she hadn't paid much attention when he ordered, her mind on other matters. That he remembered her preferences softened something inside. She lifted the next lid. A seafood platter with prawns and other delicacies, another thing she could eat.

"And kebabs for me," he said when she reached the last dish. "I dare say the service is as good as at the royal palace. Commandaria?" He picked up the sweet dessert wine from the tray, a treat that had been enjoyed on the island for centuries.

They had a few hours before they had to leave for their meeting. "Sure."

She started with the dolmades, he went for the kebabs. He ate as elegantly as he did everything else. The muscles of his lower arms moved sinuously as he put pressure on the knife. His skin was tanned. Looked as if he spent plenty of time outdoors.

He looked up. Caught her watching him. Held her gaze.

"How does one become a thief?" he asked after a few heated seconds.

Her back muscles stiffened. "I'd say one either chooses the life or is born into it."

"Still, even with the born-into-it thing, there'd be a choice, I imagine."

"When you were young, were you fully aware that you could choose to stop being a prince?"

His fork hesitated halfway to his sensuous mouth, lips that had at one point been enclosed around her nipples.

She drew a slow breath, forcing a nonchalant smile onto her face.

He took his time to consider the question carefully. "You mean abdicate the title?"

She inclined her head.

"I don't suppose. But one is a prince from the moment of his birth. He is what he is long before he has intellect enough to think about it. It cannot be such with a thief."

"Infants are used as decoys, their strollers and diaper bags are handy hiding places."

"But they don't actively participate."

"They see the life. It's their earliest memory. They see it before they know right from wrong. When right or wrong is decided by daddy."

"Even so." He didn't look ready to concede. "At some point, there's a conscious choice to participate."

"If by conscious choice you mean a four-year-old fully realizing what her father wants when he pushes her through a dog door and asks her to turn the lock to let him in."

Surprise glinted in his eyes, even as his face darkened. "Four years?"

"Or even earlier."

"What kind of parent—"

She cut him off, not wanting to go there. "Maybe one who was raised the same way."

He put food into his mouth at last and chewed methodically, not looking as if he enjoyed his meal the least even though it was prepared superbly. Not that Lauryn could enjoy hers. She hated to discuss her past, even in the impersonal way they were doing it now.

"And when that child grows up," he said after a while, "does she not rebel? Surely, at one point there is some understanding."

"By that point, rumors about her might make it impossible to switch to an honest line of work, certainly not in the art world. It's too small. Everyone knows everyone."

"And yet, apparently, it can be done." He looked at her pointedly.

"If law enforcement chooses to stop all investigation and wipe the slate clean. I'm guessing that doesn't happen to everybody." *Thank God, it happened to me. Thank God.*

He dabbed a satin napkin to his lip. "Why would they do such a thing?"

"For a price."

"Such as?"

"Information on the location of a lifetime of acquisitions. For the child to betray her parent." She set her fork down and pushed her plate away as a dark ache spread in her chest.

"And the parent?"

"Got to live the last few months of his life in a hospital under proper care instead of on the run or in prison."

She pushed her chair back and walked to the window, keeping her back to the prince. She didn't want him to see the moisture in her eyes, the guilt and conflict she still felt over some past decisions. "Somehow, I don't see you betraying your family, your brothers."

"No," he remarked quietly. "But neither would they break the law to such degree that the authorities would come to me offering deals."

Outside, storm clouds gathered on the horizon, the sea choppy. Waves crashed to shore in an endless line. She watched the water, trying to quell the storm inside. Then strong arms came around her and she was pulled against the prince's wide chest, his chin resting on the top of her head as he held her from behind.

"You surprise me. Perhaps I judged you rashly."

She blinked the moisture from her eyes, then gave an unladylike snort, which didn't seem to put him off.

He turned her in his arms gently, held her gaze. His attention on her was full and undivided, mesmerizing. His head dipped.

She stood still, needing this, needing him, refusing to think of any of the hundreds of reasons why she should move away.

The moment their lips met, heat flooded her. She felt like she had when they'd swum to shore in Porto Paphos after escaping the bullets and the jellyfish field, reaching the safety of land—immense relief and rightness, a sense of security and gratitude for having found a safe haven.

For a while, she had no coherent thought in her head, and getting lost in him was bliss. But eventually the questions came. What on earth was she doing here, with this man? What did she expect to come of this? Where did she think they were heading? Sure as anything, it wasn't some fairy-tale happy ending.

She would have thought she had more sense than to become a momentary play toy for the rich, but she was proven wrong when her mouth defied incoming instructions from her brain and opened to him.

He tasted like sweet wine and felt like heaven.

She recognized danger when she saw it.

She liked him too much, that was the trouble. Really liked him, far more than any of the others. Honor was woven deep into the fabric of him. He drew her against all reason, and the strength of that frightened her as much as it thrilled her.

She pulled back, working hard to produce some righteous anger. She needed *something* to put between them. "Just like a man. Now that you want me, you're ready to forget my past and forgive everything."

Better to have him mad at her than have him in his current mood. He was dangerous when he was bent on seduction.

"I want you. I'm not going to apologize for it," he said evenly. "You don't have to be scared of this," he added.

Her chin came up. "I'm not scared of anything."

Even as he lifted an eyebrow, a smile hovered over his upper lip. He unceremoniously pulled her back into his arms for another kiss.

Chapter Ten

It had been a long time since he'd held a woman like this. And what he remembered hadn't been this raw, this urgent. Lauryn had blasted into his life like a comet, turning everything upside down, setting him on fire.

They'd fought for their lives together, outwitting thugs on that ship, even spent a few quiet moments here and there, talking about excavations on the island and the diary of the Brotherhood, shared a couple of meals, a couple of kisses. He wanted more. More of what they already had—minus the running-for-their-lives part. She *was* the most self-sufficient woman he knew, but he still hated to see her in danger. He wanted a prolonged, full-fledged affair.

He liked her and he didn't want to let her go. It was that simple for him. But knowing women and the way they couldn't help but make everything out to be more complicated than it had to be… The key was not to leave her too much time to think.

So he deepened the kiss, drinking in her sweetness as he lifted her into his arms and carried her to the bedroom, to the bed they hadn't yet shared. Now was the time. He laid her down gently and gave his hands free rein.

Running his seeking fingers and lips over her body nearly drove him out of his skin with need. She had sleek muscles, soft curves in other places, a delicious contrast.

But his appreciation for her went far beyond his appreciation for her body. He'd begun respecting her resilience on the ship and during their escape. He'd seen her intelligence numerous times since. And now he was beginning to understand some things about her, about her past. His old prejudices were fast disappearing, leaving something new behind, a yearning for companionship with someone who was very much like him in some regards and completely different in others.

But all that was still too new for him to fully comprehend let alone articulate. For now, he was content to let his body speak. And his body and hers were definitely speaking the same language.

Her silk dress practically slipped out of the way of his hands. Her breasts arched into his palms. He'd wanted to do this all day. Her nearness, her familiar behavior with him to keep up their ruse, had gotten to him on every level. She'd smiled at him as a mistress, touched him as a mistress and tantalized him beyond endurance.

Tension had gathered all day as they were together but always in the company of others. Now they were alone. And they were like two live wires placed near each other, electricity arching between them.

His haze of need was punctured only by a sharp object drilling into his hand. “What’s—”

“Sorry.” She pulled a metal lock pick from her bra and placed it on the nightstand. Then gave him a small, embarrassed smile and went on to retrieve various other objects. A small, sharp-looking switchblade came from her panties, and he winced thinking the injury that could have caused him.

“Where did you—” He bit off the rest of the question when the answer came to him. No doubt, she’d gotten her tools either from her uncle or she’d acquired them that morning when she’d sneaked out of his cousin’s estate and left him behind.

A small pile gathered by the time she was done.

“Wearing a weapon in the presence of a royal person is against the law and carries the charge of treason,” he observed drily.

She shrugged with a grin, never one to be intimidated. “You already thought I was a born criminal.”

He didn’t like the reminder. He might have been a fool to have judged her before they even met. He didn’t play the fool often, so the thought didn’t sit well with him. “Never mind. Anything else?”

She shook her head. “You?”

“Completely unarmed. But feel free to check my pockets.”

She laughed.

He slid his hands up her thighs, dragging the material of her skirt up as he went. He felt the same sensation as when he was looking at a new site, getting to know the lay of the land, anticipating peeling off the layers one by one until he found what he was looking for.

Anticipation coursed through him. He had no doubt that there was treasure in front of him, a nagging feeling that he might discover in her something more beautiful, more profound, more valuable than he'd ever expected. He took her mouth and kissed her deeply, couldn't stop kissing her.

She didn't protest. Instead, she arched her back so he could reach the clasp of her bra more easily. And there they were, her amazing breasts about to spill out for him to see, to touch, to taste.

His body hardened even more, if that was possible. He moved his head closer. He was beyond ready for her.

The phone rang, bringing a frustrated curse to his lips. Under other circumstances he would have ignored it—or smashed it against the wall—but it was his secured cell phone and they were in the middle of important and dangerous business.

He grabbed the cell from the nightstand with one hand, holding on to her with the other. Having to push the answer button pained him. "What is it?"

"News on the investigation," his brother Miklos said. "The break-in had help from the inside, as we suspected."

"Do you know who?"

"Partial recording of one of the video cameras we've overlooked has been restored. Chancellor Egon's son, Zoltan, was on it, along with an unidentified male."

He was too stunned to process his brother's words at first. Then things slowly began to fall into place. The Chancellor's son was a spoiled brat, a man who rose in the ranks due to his father's merit rather than his own. Maybe he was jealous of the amount of time and effort his father spent on the princes since he'd been chosen Chancellor.

"What does the father say to this?"

"Crushed."

He would be. Chancellor Egon took his job very seriously, to the point of being overzealous about it, which annoyed the princes on occasion, even if they appreciated his dedication for the most part.

"What else?"

"Benedek said Zoltan was definitely the voice in the catacombs."

For a moment he didn't know what Miklos was talking about, then he remembered Benedek being trapped with Rayne in the catacombs under Palace Hill after the siege of the opera house the year before. He'd always maintained that one of the rebels he overheard had a familiar voice, but could never put a name to it. They'd suspected one of the staff and backgrounds had been checked and rechecked, two men dismissed.

"So we let people go unfairly."

"Benedek is making retribution. He's in a mood because he didn't make the connection to Zoltan earlier. It clicked the second he saw the guy on the video, but—well—"

He knew what his brother wasn't saying. If Zoltan

were caught earlier, lives could have been saved. But Benedek was not at fault.

"Nobody would have suspected Zoltan. He's like a distant cousin. His father has become a pillar—"

Lauryn slipped away to lie on the bed next to him, distracting him momentarily. He focused back on the latest developments in the investigation with effort.

"So if Zoltan was involved in both the attack on the opera house and in this heist that links the theft of the crown jewels to the Freedom Council." The clandestine group of unidentified business tycoons had been working to bring down the monarchy for ages, planning to carve the small kingdom up and divide it among themselves.

Not if he and his brothers had anything to do with it, Istvan thought and said, "This explains so many things. If there's no crown, a new king cannot be crowned and confirmed." And their mother was ill enough that Arpad becoming king someday soon was a very distinct possibility.

As Lauryn had said, taking one-of-a-kind, easily recognizable artifacts like the crown jewels made little sense for their gold and gem value alone. But the theft made a world of sense if the purpose was to disrupt the monarchy.

And the crown held other power, too. Like the key to the Brotherhood's treasure, a find of historical significance, which he didn't want to go into over the phone. He didn't even want to think about the kind of war that it could finance if it fell into the wrong hands.

"Any developments there?" his brother asked.

Istvan filled him in, getting up to pace the room as he did so.

"And how is the princess of thieves?" Miklos asked at the end, after all his other questions had been answered.

Istvan walked from the bedroom to the living room and closed the door behind him. "Don't call her that."

"What would you like to call her, plain *princess?*"

He shook his head silently. The one drawback about having a close-knit family was that they felt free to stick their noses into his business anywhere, anytime. "It's not like that between me and Miss Steler."

The connection was purely physical. And intellectual. But that was it. Nothing he couldn't walk away from at the end. Not that he'd told his brothers about the physical part even. None of their meddling business.

"Because of Amalia?" Miklos asked. "Still?"

He said nothing. Because the truth was, he thought about Amalia less and less.

"You were never in love with Amalia. You know that, right?"

"I was. You go too far. Being married doesn't make you an expert on the subject," Istvan responded with some heat.

"Why didn't you marry her?"

Why didn't he, indeed. He'd thought about that many times in the aftermath of her death. "The time wasn't right." Among many other things. "And there were obstacles. She was a commoner. Divorced. There would have been a bloody fight at the palace over it. The Chancellor would have had a stroke. Mother would have had a heart attack." The reasons that seemed to have had all kinds of power in the past, suddenly sounded weak, even to his own ears.

"Here is a piece of unsolicited advice from your big brother—the time is always right with the right woman."

"If there's nothing else you have for me on the investigation, I'm signing off here." Istvan closed the phone before his brother could have pushed further.

He longed for the days when they used to share hunting stories and sword-fighting tips. Now that Miklos and Benedek and Lazlo were married and more in touch with their emotions, whatever that meant, God help the rest of them.

Janos and Miklos had met Lauryn when they'd come and taken the ship's crew back to Valtria with them. Both liked her, which made no sense at all. Janos, maybe, but Miklos ran palace security—he'd lost several of his men to the heist. He should not approve of an ex-thief so thoroughly.

Not that his disapproval would have been better. Istvan felt defensive just thinking about anyone disapproving of her. She scrambled his brain like no other, he thought as he walked back to her.

She stood next to the bed, her dress back in place, looking as if she, too, had sobered in the few minutes that had passed. She glanced at the bedside clock. "It's time for us to leave."

For the next meeting with the next criminal. And the stakes were higher than ever. "You should stay."

She gave him a stubborn look. "We've already done that song and dance."

"These people are more dangerous than I thought." He told her what he'd found out from Miklos, told her a little about the Freedom Council. "We're not facing a simple gang of thieves with a wealthy buyer behind them. The Freedom Council's sole purpose is the defeat of the monarchy and the destruction of the royal family."

"By that you mean they'll try to kill you given half a chance?"

He nodded.

For a second she held his gaze without a word, a thoughtful look in her eyes. Then she squared her slim shoulders. "All the more reason for me to be there."

A pure gesture of courage and loyalty.

He felt an unfamiliar sensation in the middle of his chest. For now, he decided to ignore it.

BELLINGHAM WAS AN AGENT, a go-between man. Berk, the guy they were meeting tonight, was a crew boss, a different animal altogether. Bellingham was a gentleman, using his high standing in society to gain connections, to wheel and deal. He had people for protection and intimidation when necessary. He wasn't the type to get his hands dirty.

Berk was the man in the trenches. He went out on heists and put his neck on the line every time. Lauryn knew his kind only too well. He had a team of rough-and-tough criminals to keep in line, keep from going rogue or trying to take over. Any one of his men could plea-bargain his name if caught, any one could slit his throat to get a bigger share of the loot.

Berk didn't invite them into his home. He insisted on meeting at a neutral location on the Turkish side of the island, at a café near a famous bazaar where he had enough of his armed men watching to make minced meat out of them at the first wrong move. Caution was Berk's middle name. That and shooting first, apologizing later was what kept him alive.

"Does your buyer have a price range?" he asked, drawing from a water pipe. They were sitting over a plate of sweets and strong, unfiltered coffee.

The man had watery brown eyes and a sparse beard that covered only the tip of his chin, the scraggly hairs a few inches long, coming together at the end in a spike. Tattoos of Turkish script covered his lower arms. He wore an eggplant-colored suit and leather loafers that had pointy toes.

"For the right piece, he'd pay the right price," Istvan said as Fernando.

"And the right piece would be something extravagant."

Istvan nodded. "Something truly one-of-a-kind. For a private collection that's never been seen by outside eyes."

"Maybe he has something in mind and would like to commission a job?"

"He's heard about a recent job with several items he might be interested in."

"Commissioned by another collector?"

Istvan shrugged.

"The original buyer would be disappointed if he didn't get what he paid for. Bad business all around."

The two had been talking like that for an hour, hinting much, saying little as Lauryn patiently sat by. The market buzzed around them, people coming and going, shopping, drinking, making deals. Women, too. Some in Western outfits, others veiled. Coming from Turkey, Muslim conservatives were gaining ground on the north side of the island. Only a small foothold, though. Nobody gave her any trouble for her clothes or for sitting with two men, although, knowing what it would be like here, she had added a large, dark blue silk shawl to her outfit. She had draped it loosely over her head and shoulders when they'd arrived.

Directly next to the café was a spice stand, a perfume stand on the other side where scents were mixed on the spot, one-of-a-kind for each customer's taste. Clothing shops took up one full row, silks and damasks in every color of the rainbow. Another alley was dominated by carpet dealers, selling everything from four-hundred-year-old museum-quality pieces to the latest designs. Copper dishes were sold yet in another place. And leather, and everything that can be made from the material, in several shops within sight.

She'd been pretending to pay a great deal of attention to the shopping, leaving the men to talk. But it seemed the talk was going in circles at this stage. She turned her attention to them and snuggled up to Istvan. He ignored her for a while, then pushed her away.

She put on a hurt look, then shrugged and cozied up to Berk, linking one arm through his, smoothing a hand down his lapel. "Can I offer you more coffee?"

He cast an amused look at Fernando/Istvan. Then nodded.

She served him, but didn't pull away when she was done. The thunder in Istvan's eyes looked award-worthy as he pulled a wad of cash from his pocket and tossed the bills at her. "Go shopping."

She bumped into Berk as she slid off her chair, flashed him an apologetic smile. To Istvan she gave a look of defiance, but then took the money and walked away to explore the bazaar.

On her way, she passed a table where Istvan's two bodyguards sat incognito, although she was sure Berk had picked them out as soon as they'd arrived, which was fine.

She went to the candle maker first and bought a chunk of beeswax. Then a length of silk the color of her eyes. Next she visited the leather shop where she selected a supple bodice that laced up in the front, a risqué piece made for tourists. This she took into the dressing room.

She glanced through the crack in the curtain and for a second watched the man who'd been following her all along, one of Berk's goons no doubt. Tall and bulky, he looked the quintessential seedy tough guy, with a scar running along his cheekbone, a bump in his nose where it had healed badly after a fight and greasy hair combed back from his eyes.

She cast the bodice aside, took the keys she'd lifted off Berk and pressed them into the chunk of wax, then cleaned them off to make sure nothing stuck to them. Next came the papers she'd lifted from the man's pocket. She used her cell phone to carefully photograph each page. Then she put everything away and carried out the bodice. She made a show of bargaining, as was expected, but ended up leaving the thing behind.

Her work done, she walked around some more, politely refusing vendors who did their level best to lure her inside their small shops, calling loudly and offering the most incredible deals. She moved within a hundred feet of where Istvan and Berk were sitting, making a game of picking out Berk's men who were standing guard at regular intervals. She found almost a dozen and made a point of remembering their faces. They were his crew, the ones he would send after her and Istvan if something went wrong. It was better to be able to recognize them from afar.

When it looked as if Istvan and Berk were finishing up, she weaved her way back to them, stopped behind Berk and touched his shoulders, smoothed down his lapels, gave the man a sugary smile. "I love your country. Everyone is so nice."

Istvan stood up so quickly that his chair nearly tipped back. "You know how to find me," he told Berk, then grabbed Lauryn's elbow and dragged her along without a word. His steps were controlled, as was the emotion on his face, but enough tension radiated off him to tell everyone who watched that he was displeased with his woman.

The gazes of Berk's men followed them, some looking on with an amused smile.

Then one looked toward Berk's table. Some silent communication must have passed between them because the man began walking down an aisle parallel to theirs, keeping them in his sight.

ISTVAN WATCHED LAURYN come out of their hotel bathroom, again in those sensible pajamas, and go straight to the table to pour herself a glass of water. He was still fully dressed, although resting comfortably, his arms under his head as he reclined on the bed, his legs crossed at the ankles. They'd had a productive day, all in all. They both deserved a break.

He glanced toward the window. The last time he'd checked, Berk's goon was gone. He let the guy follow them back to the hotel. Let Berk have that information, let him think he had the upper hand and that Fernando and his guards weren't as sharp as they thought.

The chunk of beeswax had been picked up by his backup team, the keys already being made. The copies of the two pieces of scrap paper in Berk's pocket lay on the nightstand. On one there was an address. He'd already sent a man there to check it out. A tailor shop, not much more than a small room with a window front, his man had reported after the premises had been entered and searched. Nothing suspicious had been found.

"How did I do as the misbehaving mistress?" Lauryn brought the glass of water over and set it on her nightstand.

"You have misbehaving down pat. The mistress part needs work." He sat up and reached out and pulled her down to the bed.

She moved away from him, putting some distance and a throw pillow between them. "Listen. About this afternoon..."

Thinking about that afternoon put his body on alert and then some. Sitting on the bed with her and thinking about their passionate kisses kicked the heat up another notch. "I agree. It's high time we finished. I apologize for the interruption."

She threw him a look of exasperation. "You know that's not what I was about to say."

His body was buzzing with anticipation. As usual, her seductress act had gone only too well. Her touching him had filled him with need. Her touching Berk had filled him with thoughts of murder.

"Anyway. About this afternoon..." She looked away. "That was a mistake."

"Says who?"

"Reality and common sense."

"Both overrated."

"You can't be involved with someone like me." She turned back to him and folded her arms in front of her. "Think of the press."

He'd already thought of that. Anyone involved with the royal princes came under a magnifying glass. Her past, her family, would never stand up to scrutiny. They'd crucify her. And Chancellor Egon would crucify him for the bad press. More than ever, the monarchy had to be beyond reproach. The Freedom Council stopped at nothing to malign the royal family and turn the people against them, stooping to outright lies if needed. Lauryn's past, even if nothing more than rumors, would be used against them mercilessly.

He rarely railed against the confines of his title, certainly not like Lazlo and some of his other brothers. But he did now. Something to be dealt with later. He swiped the pillow from between them and pulled her close, pulled her down to the bed with him and settled her in his arms, kissed her temple, then the tip of a small, pink ear. "I don't see any press in sight."

She turned her head, but she didn't move away. "You want a temporary mistress."

"I want you, any way you're willing."

"Since when?"

"Since you broke the Brotherhood's code." Probably even before. Possibly from the first moment he'd set eyes on her, but he thought telling her that might give her too much power.

She struggled with a smile as her eyes opened. "You're impossible."

"I've been called worse."

"I bet." She pulled away to pick up the paper that held the information she'd lifted from Berk. The address was a dead end, but she'd also photographed some kind of a drawing.

"What do you think it is?" he asked.

"A map, but of what?" She traced the lines. "Could be roads and hills. Could be a map of the early Christian catacombs right here in Paphos."

"Could be a map of hallways inside a building."

"We need at least one point of reference. Without that, the map is no help whatsoever." She put the paper back, frustration drawing small lines around her full lips, lines he wouldn't have minded kissing away.

He reached out to fold his fingers around her slim wrist and pulled her closer.

"I can't do this," she said, her voice pained.

"Why?"

She looked as if she wasn't going to answer, but then she said, "There is something here." She drew a slow breath, looking away from him. "At least for me there is. If I open this door, it's going to hurt to walk away."

"Then don't." He caught himself as soon as he said the words. What the hell did he mean? Damned if he knew.

"I'll have to. Sooner or later. We live in different worlds."

He hated that she was right. Because, to be honest, there was something here for him, too. A pull he might have underestimated earlier. That she could coolly analyze the situation and so easily walk away from what could be burned him.

"I'm not sleeping on the couch tonight."

She moved all the way to the other side of the bed and turned her back to him. "Suit yourself."

Two hours later, he was still staring at the ceiling, which was just as well. At least his mind wasn't fuzzy from sleep when his phone rang.

The head of the team he'd left at Alexander's estate was on the line. They were following up on a number of things, as Istvan had requested.

"Our man who was following Berk called in. The guy went straight to Canda in Limassol. They hopped into a car and headed off toward the countryside," he said.

Canda was another possible link on Cyprus on their list. "Are they being followed?"

"We have two men on them. The one who shadowed Berk and the one who shadowed Canda. They'll report back to me as soon as there's any change."

"Where are they now?"

"Five kilometers from Dali."

He was dragging his clothes on already. "I'm coming."

"Me, too." Not surprisingly, Lauryn already had one of her Catwoman outfits on, blinking the sleep from her eyes, running her fingers through her copper hair to tame it enough for a ponytail.

He didn't have time to argue as she grabbed the sketchy map and shoved it in her pocket. He rapped on the door to alert his guards in the adjoining suite. They caught up while Istvan and Lauryn waited for the elevators. Probably slept with their clothes on, judging by the wrinkles.

They took two cars for safety. Having backup could come in handy. He turned on the GPS and contacted the man who'd been following Berk. "Anything new?"

"They drove into Dali and pulled into a courtyard. Not sure what happened in there, but they came out with a black van and backup."

"How many?"

"Two jeeps with four men in each. Could be more in the back of the van."

"Heading which way?"

"North."

"Morphou Bay," Lauryn said once he'd hung up.

"Probably." If his asking around spooked the thieves because they had something to hide, they could be getting ready to move the artifacts off the island. He couldn't allow that to happen. Syria was too close, just a boat ride away, so was the African coast. It would be all too easy for the thieves and the crown jewels to disappear forever.

It started to rain, a rare event in the summer. The phone rang. He pushed the on button.

It was one of his men who followed the two crew bosses. "They pulled over and got out. They're walking into the woods."

"Where are you?"

"On the main road to the bay. You'll see the cars. We're going after them."

He hung up, then called the investigative team at Alexander's estate, gave them the location and ordered them to meet him there as soon as possible. Then he stepped on the gas. "There are guns in the glove compartment," he told Lauryn. "Take what you need and get ready."

"I'm not much for weapons." She opened the compartment gingerly.

Great, an ex-criminal who didn't like violence. He should have figured. She was unusual in every other way, as well. And he would have lied if he said he didn't like that about her. She had a lot of layers, a lot of secrets to explore and investigate. He would enjoy discovering what lay at her core, as much as he enjoyed discovering the secrets of the earth. His favorite activity was peeling back layers. He had a feeling he would never be bored with her around.

But to have her around, first they had to survive the night.

He watched as she hesitated over the weapons. "For self-defense," he told her, but she didn't look reassured.

She took the smallest one, handling it in a way that told him there was very little chance of her ever firing it, which was fine. He didn't plan on putting her in harm's way. He would leave her in the car.

Soon the vehicles by the road came into sight. He parked farther down, in the cover of an abandoned shack, then called his men, who were already hidden in the woods, for an update.

Neither of them picked up.

He called again.

Nothing.

The muscles in his shoulders grew tighter and tighter, as he waited. And still nobody answered.

Chapter Eleven

"I'm not staying in the car," Lauryn told the prince before he could have told her to.

"It'd be safer," he argued without any heat, preoccupied with worry because his men weren't answering his calls, and also smart enough to know that nothing could convince her.

Good. She liked smart men. That her feelings for him were rapidly moving beyond "like" she ignored for now.

"As it would be safer for Your Royal Highness to remain safe." She used his official title to remind him who he was and what his life meant not only to himself but to others. She better remember, too, and not sink too far into some imaginary fairy tale that could never be real. "We could wait for backup to get here."

"You should."

She glared at him through the darkness. The headlights had been cut as soon as they'd arrived. The only illumination came from the moon above and little of that with rain clouds drifting through. At least it had stopped drizzling.

There were four of them, including Istvan's two guards. A dozen men would be coming from the estate where the original war room had been set up. Lauryn figured they couldn't be more than an hour behind them.

"Spread out?" she asked.

"Stick together," Istvan answered.

And soon she realized why as the guards took up protective positions around him. They were probably under order not to let the prince out of their sight.

They moved forward quietly through the woods. There was hardly any light at all as they walked, the trees filtering what little moonlight the clouds let through.

"I have a penlight," she offered, digging into her pocket.

"I have my lighter, but even that's too dangerous." Istvan kept moving forward. "We don't want to alert them that we're here."

She could barely make out the tree trunks, let alone the path. Their only chance of finding the men was catching sight of their lights up ahead, but even after long minutes ticked by, they saw nothing.

Then the guard who led the group tripped and swore under his breath. "Careful here." He bent and looked at the boulder in their way. A strange-looking boulder.

Not a boulder at all.

"Man down," the guard clarified.

Istvan stepped forward. "Ours?"

A second passed while the man checked the body, peering closer, tilting the face to the dim moonlight. "Yes."

"We'll come back for him." Istvan's voice was tight.

He took her hand and helped her over the body, and she let him even though it wasn't necessary. She was used to getting around in the dark and moving around obstacles.

"One of the men could escort you back to the car," he offered.

She considered it for a fraction of a second. She'd been a thief, sure. But she'd avoided violence all her life. The sight of it never failed to shake her. She would have to get over that tonight. "No, thanks." She hung on to his hand.

Soon they came to some sort of meadow that was dotted with rocks, some the size of beach balls, others taller than a man. Then the path went from dirt to paved with small rocks. They came to an even flatter area after that. No boulders here, but partially collapsed walls cordoned off by construction tape and a posted sign.

Istvan let her go as he passed his guards and moved up to the sign, then sounded out the letters of the Greek alphabet. "It says the site is protected by the Ministry of Culture."

"A historic ruin," she guessed and looked around, wondering from what period. She spotted an arch that gave it away. "I think Roman."

Due to the economic crisis that hit tourism hard at tourist paradises like Cyprus, many excavations on the island had been halted, awaiting better times and sufficient funds. Many sites stood deserted like this one. They'd seen two on their drive to her uncle a few days before.

Istvan moved ahead, but she grabbed for his arm after a few steps to stop him. She pulled the sheet of paper from her pocket. Of course, they couldn't see anything written on it in the dark.

"All right. Get out that penlight." Istvan directed her toward a partially excavated wall and squatted, pulling her with him. Then he told the men to surround them and block the light as much as they could from the side that wasn't protected by the wall.

She produced the penlight from her shoe. It was about the size and shape of a slim lipstick and cast its light no farther than a foot, but for their purpose, it was perfect.

"If that's the path and this is the boulder and over there is the wall—" Istvan pointed at the marks.

"Then we have to go that way," she finished.

Another thirty minutes or so passed before they found their destination, an excavation shaft they would have never come upon in the dark without the map. A man sat at the hole's mouth, leaning against a pile of stones.

They crouched and waited. Istvan was probably considering how best to rush the guy, Lauryn figured. Waiting didn't bother her. Staying still and silent was one of her specialties.

But the more she looked, the more she realized there was something strange about that guard.

Istvan turned to her with a questioning tilt of his head. She inclined her own. He signaled to one of his men to move forward. The guard did, keeping in the shadows. The others raised their guns to cover him if necessary. The man at the stone pile still didn't move.

Then the guard was there and putting a finger to the man's neck. A couple of seconds passed. The guard came back. "Another one of ours," he whispered.

Both men who'd been shadowing Berk and Canda were dead. And the backup team hadn't arrived yet. Waiting would have been the smartest thing to do. But the sound of an approaching chopper gave them motivation to hurry. The crown jewels, if they were here, could be removed from the site before backup arrived.

"That excavation shaft probably has another exit to an area that's clear and flat enough for the helicopter to land." Istvan moved forward.

Lauryn and the guards followed. He was very likely right. Excavation shafts often had multiple entry points to allow better flow for the carts going down and coming up with rubble, as well as to provide better ventilation for the workers.

The small hill could have covered an entire buried Roman town beyond the single villa that was visible.

They entered the shaft, the guards first, the prince next, Lauryn bringing up the rear. Good thing she wasn't scared of dark places. The first man walked into a wall and swore. She pulled her flashlight and passed it up front; less chance of that giving them away than the noise they made as they bumped into things. The corridor twisted enough to shield the light even as its cavernous length amplified sound.

The shaft soon linked to an ancient hallway that was made of stone from floor to ceiling, probably leading to the villa's cellar, then to a low-ceilinged room with a reinforced-steel door to one side, which was not at all normal at a standard excavation. If the authorities wanted to protect the site, they would have closed off the entrance of the shaft.

She looked at the lock, which was also not standard issue. The keys she'd lifted off Berk would have come in handy, but their copies weren't ready yet.

"Want to give it a whirl?" Istvan asked.

She got out her picks and did her best. Several minutes and some adjustments later, she smiled when she heard the small click.

The look on Istvan's face was conflicted.

"Right. You disapprove on principle." She rolled her eyes at him. "Disapproval duly noted." She opened the door and pressed inside.

An old-fashioned generator hooked to a flood lamp was the first thing they saw. Because it would have made too much noise, they didn't turn it on. Her flashlight was used instead, along with Istvan's lighter.

A dozen or so crates occupied the underground room, some full, some empty. Istvan rushed to the closest, tipping up the lid and lowering his lighter, victory in his voice as he said, "The war chest."

They immediately went to check the rest, not an easy task with what little light they had.

"Most of what was stolen from the treasury is here," he told them after a while, but his shoulders were sagging.

"Except?" she asked in a low voice, standing near him, already suspecting the answer.

"Except what was in the special vault."

So they were still missing the crown jewels.

He left a man with the artifacts and instructions to send the backup team after him and Lauryn once they arrived. Then Istvan, Lauryn and the remaining guard moved on to discover the rest of the shaft and the location of the crown jewels.

When, a few hundred yards later, they saw a dim light up ahead, they extinguished their own and moved more slowly and quietly. But then soon realized that the light wasn't manmade. Moonlight was filtering in up ahead. They reached the end of the tunnel; another few hundred feet would bring them back out into the open. They could even hear the hovering chopper.

They came out on the other side of the hill, and spotted a road nearby with a canvas-top truck and a dozen armed men, rifles outlined in the moonlight. The truck's back was open. Two men were working on lifting a large box, hurrying, keeping one eye on the helicopter.

Those who were not involved in the work held their rifles on the chopper. Whoever was up there was not their friend.

The standoff provided the perfect distraction. Istvan

moved forward, followed closely by the guard and Lauryn.

Then all hell broke loose as gunfire erupted behind them.

She dived to the rocky ground and rolled blindly for cover until she found relative safety in a ditch. A second later Istvan landed on top of her, knocking the air out of her lungs.

The gunfire stopped once the shooters lost their targets.

He poked his head up, not much of a risk given the darkness. "They had a lookout on the hillside. He saw us coming from the cave."

She, too, peeked out and saw Istvan's bodyguard a few feet away, lying in a pool of blood, arms outstretched. Her stomach constricted painfully. "Can we pull him in?"

She could feel Istvan's muscles tighten on top of her as he said, "He's gone."

The men were shouting around the truck, the crate was finally lifted. But then more shouting came from the same direction Lauryn and Istvan had just come from. The backup team. They burst forth from the opening and the men by the truck opened fire, and the chopper stepped into the melee, indiscriminately firing at everyone on the ground.

Istvan took aim at the chopper and missed. She couldn't have contributed if she wanted to. He was lying on top of her and showed no sign of wanting to move.

He took aim again and hit it this time. The rotors gave a grinding noise.

Unfortunately, the gunner had no intention of giving up on the battle.

Half the Valtrian guards were dead on the ground, the other half pulled back into the shaft. Berk's and Canda's men rushed in after them, desperate for cover from the chopper.

The hand-to-hand combat that ensued was bloody and fierce. Istvan kept shooting at the chopper, trying to at least stop the firing. And the bird did come down, even if it didn't crash. The pilot landed it just as the blades came to a complete halt. A half-dozen men jumped off immediately, keeping low to the ground and spreading out as they ran forward.

They were fresh to the fight with plenty of ammunition. They ended the battle at the opening of the shaft within minutes. Then they came looking for whoever had shot down the chopper.

Lauryn pulled her head back in and held her breath, gripping Istvan's shirt, thankful that they were both dressed in black, praying that he would stay very, very still.

HE HAD SECONDS. Istvan grabbed his empty gun and watched as a familiar man got out of the chopper, his face visible in the truck's headlights.

"Stay down no matter what happens," he whispered to Lauryn, then pried her fingers off him and stood from the ditch, threw aside his useless weapon and walked forward, bellowing, "Bellingham!"

"Stand down! Put away your weapons!" the man ordered as he sauntered closer, holding his own pistol in front of him. "Well, well, Your Highness."

He stopped in front of the man and kept his hands up, his mind working furiously as he reassessed their meeting. "You've known all along?"

"Only since Fernando was arrested this afternoon in Buenos Aires." He laughed. "Good show, by the way. I've been asking questions and learned that the Valtrian royal treasures had gone missing. I'm always game, thought I'd track them down and sell them to Fernando for a fair commission. But if it wasn't Fernando who came to breakfast, I had to ask myself, who could it be?"

He motioned Istvan toward the truck. "Maybe someone who wanted to retrieve the treasures? Didn't take much to sort out that Prince Istvan of Valtria hasn't been seen in public in the past couple of days. Turns out his secretary cancelled all his appointments. Once I had that information and your latest media photos in front of me..." He gave an aristocratic shrug.

"Name your commission," Istvan offered. "I'll pay it to have the artifacts back." It was likely the man had no idea exactly what he had captured from Berk and Canda. He hadn't had a chance to open the box yet. He wouldn't dream that it held Valtria's crown jewels.

"If only it were that simple. You see, I already thought about that. And then I thought, if whatever was stolen was important enough for His Royal Highness himself to come after it, how important could it be to your enemies?"

His heart sank. "You contacted the Freedom Council?"

"In a way. Turns out we have friends in common. Imagine my surprise when they said that they in fact would not be interested in the recovery of the treasure as they were the ones who ordered the heist in the first place. Impressive."

"Criminal is another word for it."

"I knew if anyone on the island had anything to do with it, it had to be either Berk or Canda. I had both of them followed all day. The only surprise was that they did the job together. Usually they'd dig each other's eyes out sooner than look at each other." The man shrugged. "I tell you, the power of love has nothing over the power of money when it comes to reconciling people."

"So now you do have the treasure and you can make the Freedom Council pay."

"Oh, here is the good part." Belligham laughed. "What they pay for what's on that truck will look like a small bonus compared to what they'll pay for a Valtrian prince."

Istvan didn't waste his breath protesting. While he'd come forward to protect Lauryn and because he knew Bellingham was too much of a gentleman to shoot a royal prince in cold blood—despite his unsavory occupation—he also knew that he wouldn't hesitate to sell one for the right price to the highest bidder.

The only thing he could do was go with the man and draw him away from the place before Lauryn was discovered.

Except that she seemed to be intent on getting herself killed, as if there hadn't been enough blood already spilled tonight. He caught a small shadow moving along the edge of the woods. He could have strangled her. He looked away on purpose, not wanting anyone to pick up on what he was looking at.

Then hope came, even if it was laced with misgivings.

Belligham had only a half-dozen men. They were hard to miss in the truck's headlights. If she found a decent enough cover, she might be able to pick them off one by one before they rushed her. She had enough bullets.

"I'll match whatever you think the Freedom Council will pay for me," he said to distract Bellingham.

From the corner of his eye, he watched as Lauryn reached a good-size boulder. He was prepared to drop and roll so any flying bullets wouldn't hit him. But Lauryn didn't stop at the boulder.

"If I let you go with the treasure, the Freedom Council will come after me. Nasty people." Bellingham shrugged. "If I give you to them along with the treasure, they'll be my grateful allies forever. At the end of the day, I think I'd feel better not making enemies out of them."

The sound of the truck's engine revving as it was put into gear drew everyone's attention.

"Who the bloody hell is that?" Bellingham whipped around. "Get after him!"

But it was too late. All they could do was shoot at the rear lights as Lauryn hightailed it out of there with Valtria's crown jewels, the heist of a lifetime.

Istvan stared after her, his hands coming down, his mind and body in shock for a moment. Bellingham's men were scrambling around, but he was too stunned to take advantage of the distraction. Then Belligham's gun came up and was aimed right at his chest. Outrage twisted the man's face.

But even the threat of imminent death couldn't stop the prince from breaking out in strangled laughter.

"I wouldn't be laughing if I were you," the man shouted.

"I'm not laughing at you, believe me," Istvan reassured him, looking after the truck. "I'm laughing at what a fool I've been."

"Your partner, then?" Bellingham's mood turned to amused. "Never trust a woman." Then he shrugged. "No bigger fool than I was, thinking the elusive Fernando was coming to my home for a visit. I was not pleased with my associate who vouched for you. My men had a chat with him, and with the old man who recommended you to him."

Istvan surged forward, but was stopped by the gun that was raised to point at the middle of his forehead. Frustration and worry tore through him. Chances were better than good that Lauryn would head straight to her uncle. If Bellingham's men were still there, she would be walking straight into danger.

And despite the fact that she'd just betrayed and abandoned him, he cared.

Chapter Twelve

Her cell phone was nowhere to be found. When Istvan had jumped on top of her in that ditch, he'd probably knocked it from her pocket. And, naturally, there wasn't a house in sight where she could ask to use a landline.

Lauryn drove madly over country roads that were even worse in the hills than elsewhere. She needed a plan. She tried not to think that Istvan might already be dead. Tried to keep in mind that she had to keep the car on the left side of the road if she didn't want to die in a head-on collision.

"What is it with island nations anyway?" she muttered to the steering wheel and smacked it for good measure. "And what is it with princes?"

She refused to worry about Istvan. He could handle himself. He wouldn't want her as backup anyway. He never wanted her as backup, only let her join him after considerable begging each and every time. Because in his arrogant princely mind, he probably saw her as nothing more than a weak woman. And he still didn't trust her, no matter that she'd been as straight as an arrow long before he'd ever set eyes on her. Probably wouldn't trust her in the future either, no matter what she did.

And she wasn't going to waste a lifetime trying to prove herself to him, trying to get something from him that she could never get.

"I'm not going to fall for His Highness, Indiana damned princely Jones," she said into the night. "Not gonna happen."

No matter how good his arms had felt around her.

No matter how well he kissed.

No matter how irresistible he was with all that passion in his voice and eyes when he talked about preserving history, or when they'd talked about great art. Passions they shared.

She was not going to lose all reason and determination, qualities she actually liked in herself, and go fall in love, damn him.

Which didn't mean that she was going to leave the prince at the mercy of his enemies.

Her uncle's monastery wasn't far, so she headed that way. He was the only person she trusted on this island. She needed him to look after the crown jewels while she went back to help Istvan, and she could use his phone to call the embassy and let them know they should send some men ASAP to the Roman ruins.

And, oh, hell, maybe she could talk to her uncle about her mixed-up feelings for Istvan, too, if they had an extra minute. An objective opinion might be what she needed. Someone to tell her that she wasn't falling in love.

She wasn't. She definitely wasn't.

The monastery came into sight at last, along with a shepherd and his flock by the side of the road who settled in for the night. The man had leaned his scooter against a dried-out oil tree. Seemed like a modern guy, probably had a cell phone, too, but now that she was so close to her uncle, she decided to make the call from the monastery where she'd have more privacy.

She pulled the truck right up to the heavy wooden gates, wrapped her head in a rag she found between the seats, making it look like a beat-up skullcap. She rubbed some dirt on her face from the dashboard where dust stood half an inch thick in places. Then she squared her shoulders like a man and beeped the horn.

A monk shuffled forth from the door next to the gate and looked sleepily at the truck, his wide face wrinkled with age. "What is it?"

"Wine delivery," she said, deepening her voice. She knew she spoke the local language with an accent, but that couldn't be helped. There were enough foreign workers on the island so that it shouldn't raise suspicion.

Back in the day, she'd often masqueraded as a boy or young man to get into places, the ruse not entirely unfamiliar or unpracticed. Plus she was inside the cab of a truck, concealed in darkness. She imagined women never drove delivery trucks to this gate. The monk would see what he'd always seen, what he was used to, what he wanted to see.

And he did. He barely paid any attention to Lauryn, eyeing the truck instead. "Nobody said anything about night delivery."

"Wasn't supposed to be night delivery. I had to change a tire. Twice. On a day when my partner is home and I ride alone. Killed my back."

At that, the monk nodded with understanding. He'd probably spent plenty of time on his knees in prayer. The man didn't look a stranger to back pain.

"The office is closed. You can't get paid until morning."

"Fine with me. I'd like to take a look at that tire by daylight before I head back anyway."

"You're welcome at pilgrim's hall. There's water to wash. Prayer's at six, then a small breakfast." He shuffled back through his door, then opened the main gate, letting the truck enter.

"I'll park in the back, by the caretaker's cottage." The familiarity would reassure the man that she had delivered here before, as well as put her closer to her uncle. She had a good idea of the monastery's layout from her uncle's letters. He'd often described his work as well as the renovations going on, financed by donations, progressing little by little.

She drove slowly over the uneven cobblestones, groaning when the cottage finally came into view. What looked like dozens of candles flickered in the windows.

A prayer meeting or some strange ritual? But why not in the chapel? Why in the caretaker's cottage? She'd hoped to find her uncle alone so she could ask for his help immediately.

She cut the engine and let the truck roll all the way to

the rock wall that edged the monastery grounds in the back. Whoever was with her uncle, she didn't want to draw their attention. She crept to the window, prepared to wait for the guest or guests to leave, yearning to see her uncle's familiar face. She'd been toughened up by life, but that didn't mean she never needed a hug, a soothing pat on the shoulder and to be told that everything would turn out okay.

She peeked in the front window and saw several monks at prayer, lit candles filling every available surface. Worry stabbed at her heart. What if her uncle was sick?

She would talk him into taking Istvan's offer and moving to Valtria. If Istvan said he would protect the man, then he would. Her uncle was getting old, he shouldn't live in a spartan hut that didn't even have running water and precious little heat in the winter. He looked much younger than his age, but he was well into his sixties. Too old to work as hard as he still did, keeping the grounds for a place as big as this. At one time the monastery was the only place where he was safe. But now that he had other choices, she wanted him someplace where he could live the rest of his life more comfortably.

At least in Valtria she could visit him anytime and spend time with him. Here, they were restricted to brief visits, the two of them standing outside the gate. She moved toward the back window, which she guessed to be the bedroom.

More monks in there, heads bowed as they prayed

silently in the light of dozens of small flickering flames. The bed caught her eye. Empty. Not sick then, she thought as relief filled her. Then someone moved and she spotted the table that had been dragged in from the kitchen. A long dark cloth covered the top where a body lay dressed in black, the hands folded in prayer.

Her fingers flew to her mouth to stifle the sob that tore from deep in her chest. She didn't have to guess what her uncle had died of. There were enough candles to illuminate his face, which had been beaten bloody. A glimpse was all she had, then her eyes filled with tears and she could no longer see.

Dozens of questions flew through her mind, but only one explanation came. They'd been followed here. Her uncle had been interrogated, then killed. By Bellingham? By the Freedom Council?

She sagged against the wall and cried silently, sobs racking her body. Grief pulled her to collapse to the ground. She'd brought Istvan here. She'd brought trouble to her uncle's doorstep. A cat came around the corner of the cottage and sidled up to her. She pulled the animal onto her lap and buried her face in its soft fur. Part of her wanted to lie down in the dark outside that window and cry herself into numbness. But the bad guys still had Istvan.

She swallowed her tears. She would be damned if she let them do the same thing to him.

"I love you," she whispered to the glass. "I'll always love you. You'll never be forgotten." Then she let go of the cat and as carefully as she'd come, she stole back into the darkness.

Twenty minutes of searching the grounds, moving in the shadows, and she found the office. The lock was as old-fashioned as the rest of the place and proved no impediment at all. She was inside with her usual speed.

She went straight for the phone, called international directory assistance and asked to be put through to security at the Valtrian Royal Palace.

"Security office," a man responded.

"I need to talk with Prince Miklos immediately."

"I'm sorry, ma'am, he's not available, could I help you?"

The patronizing voice made her see red. "I'm not some lovesick teenage fan, for heaven's sake. Prince Istvan's life is at stake. And so are the coronation jewels that were stolen," she added, knowing that wasn't public information.

Another voice came on the line immediately. "Prince Miklos here. Who is this?"

"Lauryn Steler. I have the crown jewels." She gave the name of the monastery. "And I know where the rest of the stolen treasure is, but your brother is in grave danger." She explained the scene the last time she'd seen him.

"We're on our way. I'm requesting local assistance in the meantime. You stay at that monastery and be safe. I'll send an escort for you and the crown jewels."

"Hurry." She hung up and exited the office, leaving everything as she'd found it, locking up behind her. Then she went back to the monastery wall and traced it until she came to a spot that was easily scaled and out of the way enough so she wouldn't be seen by anyone who might come from or go to her uncle's vigil.

Her eyes refused to dry, which made looking for handholds difficult. Half the time she went by feel, but she made it to the top. She paused there, looking toward the cottage and the flickering lights in the windows. She felt more alone than she ever had before.

Her uncle had been the last of her family.

She whispered a prayer for him, then jumped off the wall on the other side and headed straight for the sleeping shepherd.

Her old self would have taken the scooter, not wanting to be seen. She marched straight up to the man instead, not bothering to quiet the dog that immediately ran toward her, barking.

"I need your help," she said in Greek. "It's an emergency. I have to go help a friend. Right now. Immediately." She pulled money from her pocket and pointed at the scooter.

The shepherd wiped the sleep from his eyes and quieted his dog. "Go help your friend." He nodded toward the scooter. "I'll be here when you bring it back."

She thanked him and got on the road, knowing her chances of finding Istvan where she'd left him were one in a million. Hours had passed since she'd left. She didn't know how bad the damage had been to Bellingham's chopper. They might have been able to fix it and get it up in the air. And in any case, there were plenty of cars on the other side of the woods to use as getaway cars, Prince Istvan's and his guards' included.

Tears filled her eyes anew, making it difficult to see the road. She blinked them away. She couldn't bear the thought of losing Istvan, too, of never seeing him again.

And she knew without a doubt why that was. Because despite all her best intentions and protests, she had fallen in hopeless and unrequited love with the prince.

HE WAS IN A CRUMBLING dungeon, part of a half-collapsed fort left from the time of Turkish occupation. He was tied like a hog and suspended from ropes hanging from the ceiling. The result was that his arm was about to fall off and every small move he made to seek a little relief sent him swinging, activating his motion sickness.

He still had the pearl bracelet thing Lauryn had made for him, in his pocket, had been carrying it around for some reason, although he'd meant to give the pearls back to her. Of course, he couldn't reach his pocket.

The room was spinning with him, his stomach in his throat. He was hard-pressed to think of a time when he'd been more miserable, and his physical condition was only half of that misery. He was worried about Lauryn, bursting with anger and frustration that he hadn't been able to get away and go after her.

Bellingham had left with the rest of the royal treasure, giving him over to his goons to be taken away. That had been over three hours ago. He'd had human contact only once since, when the goon's leader came in to tell him that Bellingham had sold him to the Freedom Council, a representative of which was on his way to confirm that he indeed was the prince and witness his killing.

He was no longer mad at Lauryn for leaving. He was glad she'd taken off and hadn't been captured by Bellingham. His most fervent wish was that she hadn't been captured by anyone else either. She might have proven herself a thief at the end, her upbringing proving too difficult to resist, but had she stayed, she would be killed along with him.

He half convinced himself that she wouldn't go to her uncle. She had to know that it would be the first place he'd look for her if he got free.

The door of his prison opened. He twisted his body to look, the motion sending his rope turning in a slow circle. He swallowed the nausea and swore under his breath.

"Not how I imagined our next meeting, Your Highness," the man who'd come in said, shining a flashlight in Istvan's face.

"Richard Kormos," Istvan called him by name. He knew the man by reputation more than personally, although they'd met at receptions given by the Valtrian Business League. Kormos was one of the most prominent businessmen in the country, owning all the most important coal mines in the north of Valtria and several others all over Europe.

Kormos was a short guy with a trim body that spoke of strict discipline, sharp eyes, a beak nose and a forceful voice that went with his forceful personality. The business papers often wrote about his Napoleon complex.

He was not a representative of the Freedom Council, Istvan realized at once. He was one of the three mysterious founding members, all wealthy men whose identity he could only guess until this point.

"What do you want?" he asked the man, already knowing the answer, but wanting to delay until he could figure out how to escape.

"The same thing you do. My own country. Hardly seems fair that I can't have it just because I wasn't born a prince. I mean, other than being born to the right mother, what have you ever done to deserve it, Your Highness?" He spoke the words *Your Highness* like a curse, with a sneer.

The three founding men of the Freedom Council sought to destroy the monarchy, break up the country along ethnic lines and create three small republics that they would rule, adjusting laws and the constitution to their liking.

"I love my country," was Istvan's only response. If he was to be dead soon, that was one of the last things he wanted to say.

"You can guard it from the afterlife," Kormos mocked him.

"You really think you can get away with this?"

"If I didn't, would I have shown you my face?"

That question didn't require an answer, so Istvan said instead, "Harm my family and my people in any way, and I *will* haunt you from the grave."

"We'll cross that bridge when we come to it." He gave a superior grin as the handheld radio clipped to his belt crackled to life.

"We're ready. Over."

"Give me a second to get out. Wait for my word. Over." He backed toward the door as he addressed Istvan again. "A shame these wonderful old sites being abandoned for lack of funding. The weather. The rare earthquake. It's no wonder they're falling down. Take this splendid fort for example, Your Highness. Hardly any of it is standing. Nobody will be surprised if those few remaining walls collapse. We did have that rain. The ground moved. A terrible accident."

He sounded so pleased with his plan that he could barely contain himself from taunting the prince. "I don't imagine the economy will recover anytime soon. When it does, they'll have other things to do first before they return to restoring old piles of stones in the countryside. By the time they find you, if they ever do, there'll be nothing more than bones. They might do DNA testing and it might connect those bones to a prince who'd disappeared years before somewhere on the island. Then again, they might not. By then, your people will have new leaders and you will be forgotten."

He worked the ropes at his wrists furiously, no longer caring about the swinging. "My people will not bend mindlessly to your evil rule. I have faith in them."

"How touching. I've never known this emotional side of Your Highness. I must admit you always looked cold and distant at those state dinners. Anyone else you want to voice your royal love for before I leave?"

It seemed foolish, he didn't even know why he was doing it, but he said, "I love a thief named Lauryn." He wanted those words said if he was about to die, if this was the end.

"Not that I know who you're talking about, but I can—" Kormos stopped talking and fell forward, his head knocking against Istvan's knees. Blood rushed out the back of his head.

Istvan looked up, trying to see who was coming in behind him.

"Take it back," Lauryn said, tossing the bloody stone in her hand. "Or I'm not saving you."

"You don't want me to love you?" He'd never been as happy to see anyone. He felt downright giddy, which didn't mix well with nausea, but he worked with what he had. "Most women would take that as a compliment. You do know I'm a prince?"

"This is a tight place. With your ego and all, I'm not sure there'll be enough room for all of us and I need to come farther in. I wasn't talking about the love part." Her cheeks turned pink.

His head was spinning. "May I inquire, then, what you want me to take back?"

She moved with some impatience as she cut his ropes. "The thief thing."

He rubbed his wrists, turned Kormos enough to grab the man's radio. Then they were heading out through one of the many dark tunnels, but he grabbed her arm and stopped her, turned her to him. "I take it back thoroughly," he said and kissed her.

And realized in that moment that he did love her with a love that didn't slowly creep up on him unnoticed and turn a friendship into something more as he'd always assumed would someday happen to him, as he'd hoped would happen with Amalia at some point.

He barely knew Lauryn, he reflected as they began running again, but he felt as if he knew everything important about her. And he knew without a doubt that he couldn't live the rest of his life without her.

Once they cleared the ruins, they came up to the surface, not far from the Roman villa where he'd been captured. Having major digs side by side wasn't a rarity on the island due to its rich history. Often one invading nation built on the ruins of another, which made Cyprus a paradise for tourists interested in the past.

The radio came on as they sneaked into the woods. "Are you ready? Over."

He looked back over the picturesque view the ruins painted in the moonlight—four hundred years of history. "I killed the bastard myself. No need for the explosives. Over."

"It's all set up," came the protest. "Over."

"He's dead."

"Are you out and clear? Over."

"I am."

The next second, a small charge blew. Not big enough to be noticed with the nearest houses being miles away and people asleep in the middle of the night, but big enough to bring down the already-unsteady structure.

"That was a terrible thing to do." Lauryn looked as if she might cry, staring wide-eyed at the dust cloud that was rising, aghast at the willful destruction.

He felt equally stricken, hating to see history destroyed, but there was nothing they could do now. "Come on." He tossed the radio and took her hand. "We're done here."

But, of course, they weren't. Two men rose from the darkness, guards who'd been securing the perimeters. He was furious enough, after all that had happened, to go after them barehanded. He was fed up, fed up to the limit. He grabbed the rifle of the first and shot the bastard in the head without thinking, and with another well-aimed shot took care of the other even as he heard big trucks coming down the road that led through the woods. He aimed the weapon in that direction.

"Get in cover. And this time, stay there no matter what happens to me," he ordered Lauryn.

"That might be Miklos," she said, staring wide-eyed at the destruction he'd wrought.

"How?"

"I called him before I left the crown jewels at the monastery."

"With your uncle? But I thought—"

She told him what had happened to her uncle then, her eyes filling with tears. She stumbled. He picked her up in his arms.

That was how he met the first truck, with Miklos behind the wheel.

"Need help?"

"I'm good. You've got a chopper?" He thought he'd heard the sound of rotors earlier, figured it might have been Bellingham leaving, but they were high enough now on the hill so he could see Bellingham's bird still on the ground where it had been shot down. He must have called another truck to carry away the treasure.

"Where there are no trees," Miklos told him. "If you're already handled this yourself—" he looked behind Istvan "—I'm going to be very disappointed."

"Cheer up. Bellingham's and Kormos's bastards are running all over the countryside. Go to it."

"Who's Bellingham? Kormos as in head of industry Kormos?" His brother's eyebrows went up. "Never mind. You'll tell me later. No time to waste." And he directed his truck, filled to the brim with Valtrian Royal Guards, around them to tear down the path. The other vehicles followed.

"I'm sorry about your uncle," Istvan said when they were alone again.

"You can put me down. I can walk."

"Mind if I carry you anyway? It brings home the point that you're here with me and safe."

She tightened her arms around his neck and leaned her head against his chest. "Whatever he'd done in the past, he was a good man. He was different from my father. He did have a conscience. He tried to atone for the things he did. He helped me so much in the past couple of years. I have nobody left." Her voice broke.

"You have me."

"All the way to the chopper?" She went for sarcastic, knowing, as he did, that their time together would soon have to come to an end.

And he knew suddenly that he couldn't accept that. Couldn't let that happen.

"All the way to the chopper, then all the way to forever," he said and kissed her again.

Epilogue

Istvan watched Lauryn as she straightened, covered in mud from head to toe, in workman's overalls. She was the most beautiful sight he'd ever seen.

She'd put together the materials for the exhibit for the Getty, but hadn't gone back. Chancellor Egon was traveling with the Valtrian treasures.

She gave a soft grunt. "It's the curse of the Kerkay brides."

"To be loved beyond reason by their husbands?" he inquired.

"To become pregnant the moment they say the words *I do*." She set aside the small pick she'd just broken and reached for another tool in her bucket.

"Pregnancy suits you beautifully. You glow."

"We call that sweat down in the lower classes." She braced her lower back with her hands, her belly protruding from an otherwise slim frame. "I'm as large as a prehistoric whale."

"You're pregnant with twins. They run in my family." He was exceedingly pleased with himself.

"I don't know how much longer I can help you."

He put down his pail and strode over to her. "I'll set up a golden throne for you in the shade and present you with binoculars encrusted with rubies, then you can watch the dig in comfort." They were close to finding the treasure of the Brotherhood, had spent part of their honeymoon deciphering the codes cleverly hidden in the decorative patterns of the royal crown.

"At least you know me well enough not to try to talk me into staying home."

"Soon we'll be one of those couples who finish each other's sentences," he teased her.

"Sickening," she groused, but her grin ran from ear to ear.

"Beyond appalling." He couldn't have been happier. He pulled her to him and kissed her gently.

"I still can't believe they let you marry an alleged thief," she said on a dreamy sigh when they pulled apart.

"I married a heroine. The woman who saved the coronation jewels."

Not one item had been lost, which was a miracle. Miklos was still hunting the last of the bad guys on the island, working with the local authorities, to make sure something like this wouldn't happen again.

Her eyes narrowed. "Are you saying you married me out of gratitude?"

"Having a sense of obligation is a must for a prince."

She kicked him in the shin.

He lifted her into his arms and carried her to the field tent he had set up so she could take as much rest as she needed, not that she ever took advantage of it. He laid her down on the bed. "Is it still safe to—"

"The doctor says it is. You do realize you ask me that question every single day? Never mind. Yes, you may exercise your princely rights when we return to the palace." She acted all put out, but the smile in her eyes betrayed how much fun she was having.

He kissed her again, harder this time, deeper, running his hand down the front of her overalls and undoing the buttons.

"Wait. Here?" She squealed with alarm when she realized that he had no intention of postponing anything until they returned to the palace.

"I'm a born archaeologist. I do my best work in the field."

He gave her a hopeful smile. She pressed closer. And then he proceeded to make thorough love to his amazing wife, a woman he loved above all others, the woman he would love forever. He told her so, too, just to be clear.

"I love you, too." She kissed him. "You're a prince of a man." She giggled.

She was a different person than when they'd met, loosened up a lot, learned to trust, learned to be part of a large family. Learned that she didn't have to check behind her every second because he had her back. She was just as self-assured and tough as ever, but now at times she was also completely carefree, starting to believe that what they had together was good, it was real and it was going to last forever.

When all their clothing had been removed he covered her belly with kisses. Then he moved inside her, gently, slowly centimeter by centimeter, reveling in the pleasure on her face, the way her eyes widened when he pushed all the way in.

They moved together in perfect harmony.

"Who knew we'd be so good together?" She sighed as pressure built.

"I did." He dipped his head to her puckered nipple.

"Liar."

"Insulting a prince to his face is a serious breach of protocol," he said, then proceeded to seduce her thoroughly to make sure he prevented further incidents. Even if she was right. He *had* fibbed. Never in his life could he fathom that to be truly in love and be married to the right woman could be half this glorious. It seemed insane now that he used to think that being a loner was preferable to all the work it required being a couple.

The pleasure that was building in his body was nothing compared to the joy that filled his heart to the brim.

Afterward, when they lay satiated in each other's arms, he reached for his field bag and retrieved a long velvet case and gave it to her. "I finally got this today. I was going to hold it until the twins were born, as a gift..." He trailed off. He couldn't stand the wait. He wanted to shower her with presents. He didn't agree with her frequent protests that he was hopelessly spoiling her.

"A stainless steel pick?" She'd taken to archaeology like a duck to water.

He chuckled. "Get your mind out of the ditch for a second."

She opened the case and gasped as she inspected the one-of-a-kind string of large pearls. "How old is this thing?" she asked after a minute.

"About a hundred years, give or take a couple. It was my great-great-great grandmother's." He took it from her and fastened it around her neck. The pearls shone between her naked breasts. He felt desire stir again. Bent to kiss her. "We might never leave this tent."

"Your Highness," came an urgent call from outside, ruining his hopes.

"Go away."

"We found a large stone chest."

He exchanged a glance with Lauryn. They broke records getting dressed. They were back in the ditch within minutes, supervising as the lid was removed from the stone chest with the help of a pulley. Then the way was finally cleared and they could look inside.

Instead of jewels and gold coins, the chest was filled to the brim with brittle book pages, all handwritten.

"What's this?" Lauryn was pulling on white gloves.

He'd already put his on and was taking one of the better preserved books gently into his hands, opening it to the first page, deciphering the code without trouble.

"The real diary of the Brotherhood of the Crown." He took another book and inspected it. "Along with crucial historical manuscripts that had been thought lost through wars and theft. Looks like at least some of the jewels the Brotherhood had received from their admirers had been used to pay for copying and saving our history. This is—"

"The history of the country," she said misty-eyed.

"The find of a lifetime."

"Real treasure." They smiled in unison.

"We're going to read and document all of this together. And be very careful to keep the pages out of little hands." She patted her belly. "You realize this might take a lifetime?"

He pulled her into his arms and thought about spending the rest of his life with her, working side by side, loving her. "I couldn't think of a life better spent." He kissed her, his hand caressing her swollen belly where their babies were doing backflips.

"Probably impatient to get out of there and start digging. God help the royal gardens if they take after their daddy." She was grinning.

"We'll have to put a full platoon of royal guards into service around them if they take after their mother," he murmured against her lips.

* * * * *

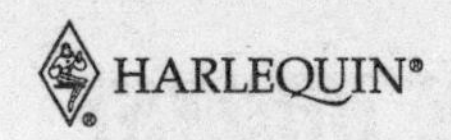

INTRIGUE®

COMING NEXT MONTH

Available July 13, 2010

#1215 GUARDING GRACE
Bodyguard of the Month
Rebecca York

#1216 COLBY CONTROL
Colby Agency: Merger
Debra Webb

#1217 THE MOMMY MYSTERY
Texas Maternity: Hostages
Delores Fossen

#1218 UNBREAKABLE BOND
Guardian Angel Investigations
Rita Herron

#1219 KEEPING WATCH
Shivers
Jan Hambright

#1220 A RANCHER'S BRAND OF JUSTICE
Ann Voss Peterson

HICNM0610

HARLEQUIN®
A Romance
FOR EVERY MOOD™

Introducing MCFARLANE'S PERFECT BRIDE
by USA TODAY *bestselling author Christine Rimmer,*
from Silhouette Special Edition®.

Entranced. Captivated. Enchanted.

Connor sat across the table from Tori Jones and couldn't help thinking that those words exactly described what effect the small-town schoolteacher had on him. He might as well stop trying to tell himself he wasn't interested. He was powerfully drawn to her.

Clearly, he should have dated more when he was younger.

There had been a couple of other women since Jennifer had walked out on him. But he had never been entranced. Or captivated. Or enchanted.

Until now.

He wanted her—*her,* Tori Jones, in particular. Not just someone suitably attractive and well-bred, as Jennifer had been. Not just someone sophisticated, sexually exciting and discreet, which pretty much described the two women he'd dated after his marriage crashed and burned.

It came to him that he…he *liked* this woman. And that was new to him. He liked her quick wit, her wisdom and her big heart. He liked the passion in her voice when she talked about things she believed in.

He liked *her.* And suddenly it mattered all out of proportion that she might like him, too.

Was he losing it? He couldn't help but wonder. Was he cracking under the strain—of the soured economy, the McFarlane House setbacks, his divorce, the scary changes in his son? Of the changes he'd decided he needed to make in his life and himself?

Strangely, right then, on his first date with Tori Jones, he didn't care if he just might be going over the edge. He was having a great time—having *fun,* of all things—and he didn't want it to end.

Is Connor finally able to admit his feelings to Tori, and are they reciprocated?
Find out in MCFARLANE'S PERFECT BRIDE
by USA TODAY *bestselling author Christine Rimmer.*
Available July 2010,
only from Silhouette Special Edition®.

SSEEXP0710